Once Upon a Cowboy

LACY WILLIAMS

ISBN: 1-942505-06-X
ISBN-13: 978-1-942505-06-8

THE COWBOY FAIRYTALES SERIES

DEDICATION

To my three princesses.

CHAPTER ONE

Early February

Just keep smiling.

Princess Alessandra, second in line for the throne of Glorvaird, meandered through the crush of bodies as the Who's-Who of New York City society mingled on the sidewalk outside a ritzy hotel. Inside the ballroom would be even worse, stuffy with the heat of so many people. The icy air chilled her skin where the slinky dress she wore didn't cover nearly enough beneath her designer coat, but inside she'd be grateful to shed her outerwear.

She detested events like these. But her royal duty demanded her presence. Her sister, the crown princess, had tasked her with forging alliances with two powerful dignitaries, which she would attempt when she could get inside. Two hours, and she could return to her own hotel, several blocks away. And rid herself of the awful, pinching heels her stylist had provided.

Paparazzi snapped pictures from behind a cordoned-off line, the flashes from their cameras whisking her to the present and out of her thoughts. Hired security milled around, looking bored. After years of being in the public eye, she was used to the presence of both.

It didn't mean the press weren't as annoying as gnats, constantly buzzing in her ear.

One misstep, one faux pas, could follow her around on the Internet for a year.

She smoothed her skirt unobtrusively and kept the smile fixed on her face.

A hand on her elbow made her pause amidst the crowd.

Her bodyguard. Tim was dark-haired and fair-complected, bulky, and more than a head taller than she. He usually faded into the background.

The fact that he'd moved in close had her pulse speeding.

"What's—" *wrong?*

She didn't get both words out before a *pop* echoed above the rumble of the crowd.

Tim's body jerked.

He fell into her. Knocked her off the precarious heels. They tumbled together. Her elbow scraped against the pavement.

The crowd rumbled. Feet shuffled in the

periphery as the other high society types didn't seem to know whether to move closer or farther away.

Alessandra struggled to separate herself from Tim, but he weighed close to a hundred pounds more than she did, and his body was heavy and unmoving. Her coat had fallen open when he'd landed atop her, and they seemed to be tangled together.

Why wasn't he moving?

"Stay—down," he gasped.

Someone screamed.

And she realized the hot, sticky substance that covered her hand where she'd tried to push him off was blood. *His* blood.

"Tim!"

Blind panic added strength to her scrambling, and at last she was able to push him off. He rolled to his back, his suit coat falling open to reveal his white shirt stained red.

"Someone—" She looked up at the blur of faces surrounding her. There was no one she recognized.

She pressed her hands to Tim's chest to try and stop the flow of blood, but more seeped up between her fingers. *No!*

"Please, is there a doctor?" she called out. In the cacophony of voices, she couldn't make out a distinct answer. "Can someone call for help?"

But as she looked down on the man bleeding out

beneath her hands, she realized it was too late. Tim's eyes had gone glassy and unfocused.

He was gone.

Someone had shot him.

He'd died protecting *her*.

Her fright didn't recede as she glanced at the faces surrounding her. Some sympathetic. Some crying, panicking now that they realized the nightmare was real. Two of the hired policemen edged through the crowd and knelt beside her.

They provided scant cover.

Was someone waiting to take another shot? A sniper? A killer in the crowd?

If she stood, would another bullet find her? Would she collapse beside Tim, her life dripping out onto the New York sidewalk?

She'd stayed crouched beside the man who'd given everything to protect her, shielded by the police who hovered near. People everywhere. Noises. The scent of blood.

She'd never felt so alone.

One thing was clear. She had to get away.

Far, far away.

~ * ~

Gideon Hale winced as he stepped off the somewhat

sheltered back porch and into the biting February wind. He'd already waved Apollo, a German Shepherd Dog, back inside to his bed in the mudroom. No use in both of them freezing their guts out here tonight.

It was after ten and the other cowhands were abed. Not him.

At least it wasn't snowing. Or sleeting. For now. The north Texas weather could change quickly, and often did.

He left the ranch house behind, his booted strides quickly eating up the distance across the yard. The moon shone above the row of elms that lined the gravel drive, casting eerie shadows. By rote, his eyes scanned for anything out of place. Until he shook himself out of it.

This wasn't Afghanistan. Or any of the top-secret locations he'd traveled to.

By the time he hit the barn, his hands were chilled inside his leather gloves. He slipped through the double doors and pulled them closed behind him.

The barn was split into two sections. One enclosed, one open to the elements. It provided shelter to the Angus cows that were his family's livelihood, allowing the mamas and babies free access to the paddock beyond.

He'd brought in two prospective mamas from the

larger, western field earlier in the day, suspecting they were close to giving birth.

This was a critical time of year for the Triple-H. Calving season. The next few weeks would determine how much of a profit they'd make this year. His family was counting on him.

And he knew it was Mother Nature, not a conscious choice, but it seemed as if the animals always gave birth on the most bitter nights of the year.

When he checked on the soon-to-be mamas, they were resting peacefully. No signs of agitation, no sign that they were close to giving birth.

Which made him suspicious. Running a herd of fifteen-hundred, they rarely went a day this time of year without several births.

So he bundled his work coat tighter around himself and went out the back of the barn, rounding the side of the structure to where the UTV was parked. It didn't want to crank, probably because of the bitter temperatures. He prayed it wasn't the battery, prayed he wouldn't get stranded out in the fields on a night like this and have to walk home.

The UTV started, and he threw it in gear, bumping his way out of the barnyard and into the field behind. The vehicle had a windshield but little else to shelter him from the open air, and he was frozen through by the time he reached the paddock where the rest of the mamas and expecting mamas were kept.

Sometimes, on nights like this, he wished he was back on the Teams. It had been blisteringly hot during their last covert mission in a place he wasn't supposed to talk about, and he'd lost several pounds of water weight. Two years ago, he'd been an integral part of the close-knit team. Had been armed and lying on his stomach on the sand next to Cash, too close to the Tangoes to whisper a joke or two, separated from the rest of their team by a few hundred yards as they waited for the order to infiltrate.

It hadn't been comfortable. And it wasn't the adrenaline rush that he missed now.

It was the camaraderie. Those guys knew him. They were like brothers.

Gideon had blown his knee out on that mission, injured himself so badly that he wasn't fit for duty anymore. And while he'd been in the hospital, his stepdad had died. Which meant his little brother and sister had needed him to run the Triple H.

So here he was. Missing his SEAL family and freezing his toes off on what might be a wild goose chase. He gritted his teeth against the thoughts. Shook them off. What he had been didn't matter now. His place was here.

He located the herd, tucked in a shallow gully. Between the UTV headlights and the fog lights rigged on the roof, he started counting.

One cow was missing. Or maybe he'd counted wrong.

Thoughts of his warm bed had him closing his eyes for a split second. Then, with a groan, he reversed the UTV and started making another pass. Hopeful he'd been wrong.

But a second count didn't turn up the cow. Gideon had worked the herd long enough to know their markings and ear tag numbers and realized this was one of the few heifers who'd been bred. This would be her first delivery.

She'd probably be fine. Cows had been giving birth since the beginning of time, right?

But the bitter cold and the fact that sometimes cows that hadn't delivered a baby before got into trouble had him stubbornly refusing to give up. A lost cow was lost money. More when you considered the calf too. His family depended on the Triple H's income. After what Carrie had been through, she deserved for him to give it his all, even if it wasn't what he dreamed about in the dark of night.

He'd take one last pass through the pasture and see if he couldn't find the heifer.

Maybe he'd get back to bed before one. If he was lucky.

CHAPTER TWO

Gideon didn't make it to bed at all.

By the time he'd found her, the cow had been in labor and was very distressed. There'd been blood, and she'd been down. He'd had no way to get her back to the warm barn, so he'd stripped out of his shirt and done what he could to assist the birth.

Turned out there was a reason she'd been in trouble. She'd given birth to twins. With the mama so weak—although she'd quickly gotten to her feet— and two calves shivering and covered in fluid, he'd known he had to get them back to the barn.

Which was a trial-and-a-half, because the mama had turned protective, fast.

It'd been nearly four when he'd finally stumbled into the farmhouse. Only to find Nate, the foreman, scrambling two dozen eggs for the rest of the hands. He'd spent a half hour discussing the day's agenda and stressing the need for Nate to send one of the hands out to check for more newborn babies in the field.

If it'd been any other day, he might've caught a combat nap, but his brother Matt was flying in on an early-morning flight, and the website showed it was on-time, which left Gideon only time for a quick shower.

Now, after a two-and-a-half hour drive to Dallas and sitting an hour in traffic, he waited in the baggage claim for his little bro.

Little.

Matt was active duty Air Force and on leave from his tour overseas. Gideon was proud of him.

And maybe a bit jealous too.

His bum knee *panged* in sympathy, and he shifted his feet, trying to alleviate some of the pressure. His eyes flicked to a TV angled from the ceiling. It was hard to hear in the echoing cavern of the luggage claim, but he caught the words "assassination attempt," and he zoned in. Apparently some European princess had gone missing in New York City. He wondered if any military personnel would be called in to help, or if the Feds were handling it.

And then he didn't have time to wonder anymore, because passengers started trickling down the escalators. Then came a flood, complete with a large family of jostling teenaged boys and a smaller family with a squalling baby and a toddler clinging to mom's pant leg. Dad pushed an overloaded stroller and looked like he wanted to be anywhere else.

And there was Matt, his fatigues and crew cut instantly recognizable among the civilian clothing surrounding him. He looked exhausted and stressed, lines fanning from the corners of his eyes. When he caught sight of Gideon, he smiled, but it was rough.

Gideon's stomach clamped into a tight ball. Something was wrong. He watched his brother's approach closely but couldn't see any signs of injury.

Then Matt was beside him.

"Hey, man." He wasn't ashamed to pull his brother into a back-slapping hug. "Good to see you." And it was. Now that he was on the other side of the deployment, he'd realized how much worry he'd put his family through while he'd been off on missions.

They both backed off to a respectable, manly distance. "You're looking pasty, old man," Matt said.

"Long night." Gideon shoved the Stetson back on his forehead. "Little heifer gave birth to twins out in the field."

Matt squinted. "And you had to help?"

Gideon shrugged. She'd been in pretty bad situation when he'd arrived on the scene, with the first calf twisted up in the womb. "They survived the night."

"How's Carrie and the little booger?" Matt asked

as they turned to follow the crowd.

"They're fine. Can't wait to see you at dinner tonight."

They moved closer to the carousel, which now spun. Luggage appeared in a slow trickle. When Matt grabbed his government-issued duffel, Gideon couldn't help looking over his brother again. Was Matt limping slightly? He couldn't be sure. His brother was saying all the right things, but something was off.

Gideon made his brother hand over the duffel— which Matt did with only a minimum of stink-eye— and slung it over his shoulder as he led the way to the parking garage.

"You hungry? Figured we could stop somewhere on the way back to the Triple H."

Matt shifted his nearer shoulder, and Gideon resisted the urge to narrow his eyes. Dislocated? Or was Gideon just being paranoid? Trying to see the worries that plagued him because he could guess what his brother had walked into over there?

"Sure, I could eat."

That was a good sign, at least.

They reached the right level in the parking garage and approached the truck. Gideon stowed Matt's duffel in the truck bed, where it landed next to the blue tarp he'd thrown over the tools he'd used two days ago to repair a section of broken fencing in one of the pastures. He'd meant to unload the tools in the barn yesterday but had never gotten around to it.

He was glad to hop in the truck and crank the heater. He rubbed his chapped hands together. If anything, it had gotten colder in the night, although he hadn't heard about a front moving through.

He felt the shift in the cargo as he backed out of the parking space and kicked the truck into *Drive*. Hadn't realized he'd used that many tools.

Matt slouched in his seat, long legs eating up the space beneath the dash.

"How long is your leave?"

"Three weeks. Maybe a month." He grunted. "Why, you need another hand for the spring cutting?"

Gideon grinned. Castrating bull calves, turning them into steers, had been his brother's least favorite task on the ranch during their growing up years. "If you're going to be a sissy about it, I'm sure the hands and I can handle it without you."

Matt leaned his head against the seat-back. "Trey still hanging around? Still mooning over Carrie?"

"I don't know about mooning. We've still got the same guys working for us. Nate, Brian, Trey, Dan, Chase. If cattle prices stay up, we'll make enough from the summer sale to buy out old man Cameron.

Maybe add another hundred head."

Matt grunted again. He'd worked the ranch, same as Gideon, and left as soon as he was of age. Same as Gideon. Neither one of them had wanted to stay on and work the ranch long-term. Only now Gideon was back, running the ranch for their family. Trying not to chafe under the small-town life.

Carrie needed him. He owed her.

"Think *Gerry's* will be too busy for breakfast?" Matt asked.

The mom-and-pop diner was halfway home, not too far off the interstate, and a popular eatery in three counties. Mama G, the proprietress, served a mean omelet.

"Might be too busy if I hadn't called Mama G on my way down and told her you were back home for awhile. She's reserving a table for you, soldier-boy."

Matt grinned, but there was something behind the smile that Gideon couldn't read, not when he needed to keep his eyes on the interstate traffic.

Over an hour later, they exited I-30. It'd be another fifteen minutes of two-lane highway to *Gerry's*. They'd covered all the small talk Gideon could stand in his exhausted state and fallen into a comfortable silence. It'd always been like that growing up. They'd understood each other, sometimes hadn't needed words.

A thump from the truck bed had Gideon glancing in the rearview mirror, then reaching up to tug the mirror down so he could see. He hadn't taken the last turn fast enough for the tools and duffel to shift. Not that much.

Was something moving back there? He hadn't seen any kind of bird come out of the sky. He'd checked that Apollo hadn't hopped up in the truck bed before he'd left the house this morning at oh-dark-hundred.

Matt had been staring out the window, but now came alert, sitting up straight. "What's the matter?" He twisted in his seat, glancing out the back window, then back at Gideon.

"Something moved in the back."

He felt Matt's skeptical stare. "Like what?"

Gideon shrugged, shifting his neck side to side. He'd been sitting in the truck for too long this morning after a long night, and his muscles were tight. "Something."

He spotted a turnout off the two-lane state highway and put on his blinker.

"Seriously?"

He glanced at his brother, brows raised. "You're that hungry for Mama G's cooking? Can't wait two minutes for me to tie down my tools?"

Matt just frowned.

Gideon stopped with a crunch of the tires on dirt and threw the truck into Park. "Just give me a minute."

Of course Matt followed him out of the truck.

He'd left it idling, but something rustled beneath the tarp even above the engine noise. Glancing at Matt over the truck bed, he reached in and rolled back the tarp to find a white-faced woman huddled beneath.

~ * ~

Alessandra was frozen through. She couldn't feel her fingers or toes, and her teeth had stopped chattering an hour ago. She'd never been so cold her teeth ceased chattering. The irony of escaping an assassin only to die of hypothermia.

She barely registered that the truck had stopped before the darkness of her covering lifted and she came face-to-face with a grizzly bear. With a jolt she realized it was a man, but with a dark, shaggy beard covering his face and long hair that fell into his eyes, he might as well have been a bear. The look in his intense, dark eyes said he'd kill her.

"Who are you?" he growled.

She tried to answer, but her lips wouldn't form words.

"She's half-frozen," said another voice. Her neck twinged when she tried to turn her head, and she strained her eyes to the opposite side of the truck bed to see another man, this one clean cut and in a military uniform, although he shared the same dark eyes as the first. Related?

Her heart pounded with fear, but she still couldn't make her muscles move. She had no strength left, not after running for thirty-six hours. She'd passed through six airports, spent most of that time hiding in restrooms and freaking out over every glance another passenger sent her way.

The first man—the grizzly bear—grunted and reached for her. She was used to everyone carefully staying out of her personal space, but she couldn't form a protest when his hand clamped around her upper arm. He tugged, and she slid across the slippery metal truck bed.

And then he hauled her bodily over the side, lifting her easily, as if she were a bag of Glorvaird apples or one of the tools that had been poking her beneath the plastic tarp.

Military-man stayed on his side of the truck.

Her legs wobbled, but she didn't fall when he set her on her feet.

Who where they? Did they mean her harm?

"L-let g-go of me." There. She'd gotten the words

out, and even with the wobble, she'd sounded almost imperial.

The grizzly bear did let go, and she had to clutch the side of the pickup and lock her knees to keep from tumbling to the ground.

She didn't like the way he looked her up and down. Not the way she was used to men looking at her. Usually they were assessing her figure, not her threat level.

She wasn't the threat. He was!

"Who are you?" he demanded. "Why were you stowed away in my truck?"

She stalled, looking away from the bear's narrow-eyed gaze and over his shoulder instead.

She'd hoped to escape the airport without being tracked by surveillance cameras, hoped that when the truck stopped, she'd be able to unobtrusively get out without anyone being the wiser.

She'd failed.

And it appeared she'd hitched a ride to the middle of nowhere. They'd stopped along a stretch of lonely two-lane road. Fields of red-brown dirt extended to the horizon in both directions. There was nothing else within eyesight. Just the two men and the truck.

No escape.

She should be worried, but right now, she felt only the same numbness that had stolen over her yesterday.

"How'd you get in my truck?" he demanded. His eyes glittered with what she assumed was anger.

"I c-climbed in. I n-needed to get o-out of the airport w-without being seen." She'd snuck down the escalators to the parking garage, hiding in a large group that seemed to be coming off a mission trip, judging by their colorful backpacks with patches sewn on. In the parking garage, the group had loaded up into two large vans, and she'd been left alone, creeping between vehicles and not sure what to do next.

Then, a scary-looking man with a shaved head had come off the elevator, and she'd panicked anew. Had he tracked her here from New York?

She'd seen the beat-up truck and the plastic blanket inside the bed and quickly jumped in and covered herself up. It could barely be called a plan. It evidently hadn't been a good one.

She was finding she wasn't very good at taking care of herself. Although at least when she'd been running, she hadn't had time to think about...

The bear must've said something else that she'd missed, lost in her thoughts. She was getting kind of foggy. She still wore the evening dress and long coat she'd had on for the benefit two evenings ago. The clothes were impractical and had done nothing to keep her warm, exposed as she was in the back of the truck.

"Gideon, get her in the truck."

The bear—Gideon—growled at the other man. Maybe he really was part-animal.

"Does she look dangerous?"

Gideon the Bear assessed her again with a long up-and-down glance. He muttered something under his breath and moved toward her, gripped her upper arm.

She tried to pull away. Too weak. He towed her to the cab, yanked open the door with his opposite hand, and practically shoved her inside.

The other man, the soldier, was getting in from the passenger side. "You need some help?" he asked, as she struggled to make her icy muscles move enough to slide in the truck.

She shook her head slightly.

There was no way to ignore the presence of Gideon the Bear behind her, and she soon found herself squished between the two broad-shouldered men. The soldier reached across and turned the knob for the heater. It was already much warmer, just being inside the truck, but the extra heat bled through her skin and into her extremities. And it felt so good.

Until her skin started to prickle. And then it didn't

feel good at all.

~ * ~

Gideon shared a look with Matt above the blonde's head as she began to shiver violently.

She was putting on a brave face, but he knew what it felt like to be so close to hypothermia—he'd been close once, on his very first mission with the teams.

When your body started warming up, it felt like tiny knives pricking all over your skin. It hurt.

Judging from the fancy dress and coat—was she even wearing stockings?—he guessed she had exposure, though the skin he could see wasn't the awful grayish-white that would indicate frostbite, or he'd be driving her to the nearest hospital.

He didn't think Matt's motives for getting her in the truck were entirely altruistic. His brother had to have known that the heat would be painful for her. No, Matt knew that now was the time to get some information out of her.

"Who are you?" Gideon asked again.

She glanced at him askance. "N-no one." Her teeth were chattering now, which he guessed was a good sign.

Matt stared at the woman.

Gideon could admit she was attractive. Striking,

with her pale blue eyes and long blonde hair. She'd looked so frightened when he'd pulled back the tarp. Like a waif in need of rescuing.

Which just raised his suspicions higher. Something was really wrong here.

Why had she targeted *his* truck?

"What's your name?" Gideon pressed. "What're you running from?" Because it was obvious she was running from something. The evening gown and coat stunk of money. And those shoes... they were impractical, skinny heels and strappy—you'd break your ankle trying to make a quick getaway. Even the faint whiff of perfume she wore smelled of money.

And for a moment when he'd pulled her out of the truck, her coat had fallen open, and he'd thought he'd seen a dark stain inside. Dried blood?

Everything about her was setting off warning bells in his head.

And then Matt raised his eyes to meet Gideon's gaze above her head again, and this time he shook his head slightly.

Gideon shook his head right back. Matt might be a trained soldier, but Gideon was an operator and trusted his instincts. He didn't know what his little brother was thinking. Coddling her?

Matt didn't back down. *I know who she is*, he mouthed above her head.

What—how?

"Can you—take me somewhere with a telephone?" the woman asked.

"We aren't going anywhere until you give me some answers."

Matt frowned at him.

She looked past him, to the door.

Let her try.

She was trapped between the two of them. No way would a lightweight like her be able to get past a former SEAL and a soldier. And anyway, if she got out of the truck, where would she go? Only one stock-hauling semi had passed them since they'd pulled over. No way was she walking far in those shoes.

"You promised me *Gerry's,*" Matt reminded him.

Gideon resisted the urge to roll his eyes. How could his brother be slave to his stomach right now? The fact that there had been a woman hiding in the back of his truck had derailed their breakfast plans.

"Let's take her with us," Matt continued, as if Gideon had already agreed. "We can figure out what to do from there."

No way.

Matt must've seen his refusal in the set of his jaw. He mouthed, *trust me.*

Gideon knew his little brother probably meant

well, but Gideon was driving. He was in charge here.

But judging by the stubborn set of the woman's chin, she wasn't giving answers anytime soon. Could Matt really know who she was?

Gideon rested one wrist over the steering wheel and glanced at the land surrounding him. There was nothing here. They had another ten miles to go before they reached the small town where *Gerry's* was located.

What was he going to do, leave her to hitchhike? He might be suspicious, but he wasn't cruel.

No way was a cab or Uber driver from the city driving all the way out to *Gerry's* to pick her up, but if they left her with a hundred bucks, it didn't count as abandoning her, did it?

What other choice did they have? It's not like he'd invited her to hitch a ride in his truck.

"Fine." He put the truck in gear and hit the gas, pulling back onto the two-lane.

Matt yanked his phone from one of his cargo pockets and played with it. Seriously, his text couldn't wait until they got this mess figured out?

The woman remained silent, rocking slightly back and forth, though her shivers had lessened.

A few minutes later, they pulled in front of *Gerry's* and found a lucky parking spot at the back of the lot—lucky because they didn't have to park in the overflow lot across the street. The sleepy little town was mostly quiet, no traffic coming down Main Street, even though *Gerry's* lot was full. The feed store two doors down also boasted a few cars in the lot, but the church and bank across the street seemed virtually empty.

He got out, motioning for the woman to follow him. "C'mon."

He saw her glance around as she slid from the truck until her feet touched the ground.

"Don't even think about it." He took her upper arm, ensuring she wouldn't try to bolt. What had her so flighty?

"I'll thank you not to put your hands on me." Her voice wasn't wobbling anymore, and that tilt of her chin... was she seriously trying to order him around?

"When I start getting some answers, we can negotiate."

Matt shot him a look as he joined them in front of the truck, sandwiching the woman between them.

Inside, the restaurant was bustling. Mama G, slightly overweight and in her fifties, must've been watching for them, because she was out from behind the counter before the bell above the door had quit ringing, her arms thrown around Matt in an exuberant hug.

Several good 'ol boys took up seats at the

counter—probably a few of them Vets. They started clapping, and soon the restaurant erupted in applause and "welcome homes," for his brother. Matt deserved it, even if they didn't know most of these folks.

And Gideon used the distraction to tow the woman to the booth against the wall with a small, handwritten *Reserved* card sitting on its edge.

The woman glared at him, but he was much bigger than she was, and she allowed herself to be nudged into one side of the booth.

He followed her in, blocking her way out.

The applause died out, and Matt approached, accepting several backslaps on his way. He slid into the opposite side of the booth and handed Gideon his phone.

The screen was lit with a picture that did look sort of like the woman sitting regally beside him, her back straight as a poker. Sort of. The phone picture showed a beautiful young woman with perfectly-styled hair and too much makeup smiling at the camera. The woman beside him looked bedraggled, her hair limp, her face pale. Definitely her.

She glared at him, and he glanced back at the phone. Read the photo caption. *Princess Alessandra of Glorvaird* at some fancy-pants reception last year.

A princess?

Suddenly, he remembered the newscast he'd caught only seconds of in the airport. This was the princess who'd been shot at in New York? Whose bodyguard had died?

How in the heck had she ended up here?

CHAPTER THREE

Alessandra watched in horror as Gideon the Bear glanced at the phone's screen. Her own picture looked back at her.

Her heart beat in her throat, threatening to choke her.

Any chance at anonymity she'd had was gone.

The question remained: what would they do now? The two strangers could hold her for ransom. Abandon her.

But the compassionate glance that the soldier sent her... Somehow, she knew the brother in military garb was on her side. Would he help her?

Gideon the Bear's head came up slowly. While he'd been suspicious and surly before, something clicked inside him as quickly as his posture changed. Where he'd been tense, now his shoulders had straightened, something tight and controlled in his actions.

"I guess you've had a hard couple of days, haven't

you?" Military-man asked.

At his words, unbidden tears filled her eyes.

Tim.

She'd tried to keep him from her thoughts. but every time she closed her eyes or started to drift off, images of his blood flowing up between her fingers played behind her eyes. He was dead.

She blinked at the images now, working to erase them.

Gideon the Bear shifted closer to her—close enough for their thighs to brush—and she tensed.

"Easy," the soldier said, his voice a low rumble that barely carried across the table. He tilted his head, and she followed his glance to a young woman wearing an apron over her T-shirt and jeans, rapidly approaching their table.

Gideon's arm stretched across the back of the booth. Not quite touching, but close enough that she felt the heat radiating from him.

She wasn't used to the closeness, to someone else being in her space, and she wanted to curl into a ball in the corner of the booth, regardless of the soldier's assurance.

"Pull your coat closed," the Bear murmured, head tilted toward her, as if they were having an intimate conversation. "It stands out, but not as bad as your dress underneath."

She didn't have to look around to know it was true. On the way in, she'd seen the older men in overalls and worn flannel shirts, the young mother with her brood in stained discount-store clothing.

She stuck out like a sore thumb.

She might not trust Gideon the Bear, but she could admit he was right.

She pulled her coat closed and crossed her arms just as the waitress reached their table.

"So you're back." It was said to the soldier with a smile, but Alessandra had grown up around politicians, dignitaries and other royals, and she easily read the tension behind the woman's expression.

"So I am." The soldier's return smile was more genuine, but still, an something underlying remained. "Life treating you right, Katie?"

"Just dandy." Only the words rang somehow false. Katie raised her order pad and pencil. "What can I get you?" While at first she'd only seemed to have eyes for the soldier, now her gaze widened to encompass Alessandra and Gideon as well.

Alessandra wanted to shrink beneath the table. If the two men had recognized her so easily, just how quickly would someone else discover her identity?

"Coffees all around," the soldier said easily. "And three of the house specials. Gideon said his girl has been begging him to bring her here for weeks.

Right?"

Gideon's *what?*

Alessandra forced a trembling smile when the waitress's gaze darted back to her. She tried not to lean quite so far away from the hulking man at her side.

The man beside her didn't seem happy with the soldier's explanation either. She could see a muscle ticking beneath his eye.

Thankfully, the waitress didn't comment, only scratched something on her order pad before she turned away. A man in a worn ball cap with a green logo above the bill waved her down before she'd gone two steps.

"Way to act natural," the soldier scoffed.

"That was probably the worst thing you could've said," the Bear returned, leaning forward slightly, over the table. "If she wants to avoid people scrutinizing her. Everyone around here knows I haven't dated in"—his furious whisper broke off as he glanced at her briefly—"a long time."

The soldier shrugged, a smirk playing around the edges of his mouth. "It's about time," he said. "You're not getting any younger."

Gideon grunted.

The waitress reappeared at Gideon's elbow, efficiently setting three cups of coffee on the table, along with a small open carafe of creamer. "Sugar's on the table." She scurried away to buss a table that had just emptied.

The soldier's gaze stayed with Katie for longer than was really necessary.

Gideon scooted Alessandra's mug closer, and she wrapped her hands around it, grateful for the warmth that bled into her still-chilled body. He nudged the creamer her way, and she took it too.

"Thank you," she murmured.

"Ah, so you can talk."

She looked up sharply at his words. His dark eyes glittered, but it was almost impossible to read his expression behind the heavy, shaggy beard.

"Gid," the soldier chided. He sent an apologetic look to her. "I think we've got off on the wrong foot. I'm Matt Hale. Gideon is my big brother. My grumpy big brother. And you're—"

"Allie," Gideon interrupted. He didn't glance around furtively or do anything that might've brought attention to them, but he practically skewered his brother with a dark-eyed gaze. "It's better if you don't call her anything else."

Allie. She experienced a flash of memory from her childhood, when she'd wanted to be "just Allie," and live with the head housekeeper.

She blinked the memory away. She hadn't thought

about that in years.

Had the shock of her ordeal caught up with her?

She let out a shaky breath. "If you recognized me," she nodded to Matt, "what's to stop someone else from doing so as well?" She sipped her doctored coffee, but the warmth didn't reach all the way inside, where she'd frozen solid when Tim had stepped in front of that bullet for her.

Matt smiled, an easy smile. Now that there was no sign of their waitress, his body language relaxed. He slouched in the bench seat, clearly at ease. "I spent all day yesterday in airports. They must've replayed the same news coverage every hour. But around here... most of the folks don't get cable or pay much attention to national news coverage. They maybe got a blip on the local nightly news."

She glanced at Gideon, who wasn't at all relaxed like his brother. But he nodded, confirming Matt's words.

"No one around here would expect to meet a"— he waved his hand her way—"someone like you. People see what they want to see."

Their confidence was something of a relief, but it didn't help with her current predicament.

"I'm U.S. Air Force," Matt said. "And Gideon is a former Navy SEAL. You might not have handpicked his truck before you climbed into it, but you've found two guys who are willing and able to help you."

Gideon mumbled something beneath his breath. He didn't seem happy to be sitting next to her.

Well, that made two of them.

The waitress made another appearance, this time delivering three steaming plates of omelets, bacon, sausage and toast.

Matt had already shoveled two bites into his mouth before the waitress had walked away.

The food smells, salty and meaty and hot, rose to Alessandra's nose. She had to be hungry.

But her body's response was off.

Alessandra stared down at her plate, wondering if she'd be able to eat at all. Yesterday, she'd been so focused on getting away from New York City, getting somewhere safe, that she had barely paid attention to her body's needs. When she'd bought a health bar from a vending machine in one of the airports she'd bounced around, she'd barely been able to stomach it, still reeling, grieving over Tim.

But now...her stomach gave an audible growl.

Matt seemed oblivious, his eyes closed as he savored the food.

But Gideon had to have heard it. He shifted slightly in the seat, his knee bumping hers in their close proximity. "It gets easier," he said in a low voice.

She glanced at him briefly, unsure how to take his meaning.

"To go on."

It didn't seem fair. She could go on eating. Go on living. When Tim would never have the chance.

But she also didn't have a choice. She had a duty to her family. To her father. To her people.

She picked up a strip of bacon and bit into it. Salty, greasy goodness exploded over her tongue. Tears pricked her eyes at both the rightness and the wrongness of being able to enjoy it.

Thankfully, both men pretended not to notice as she raised her paper napkin to her face and dabbed at her tears.

A few moments passed in silence as the three of them ate.

"What happened after you left the—the scene of the shooting?" Gideon asked, his own fork clinking against his plate.

"Gid," Matt admonished through a mouthful of food.

"If she wants our help, we need to know what's going on. Have all the facts."

She hadn't said whether she would accept their help. Her gut told her she could trust the two men, but she didn't know whether she could risk putting someone else in danger. If what happened in New

York had truly been an assassination attempt, what would keep the assassin from tracking her down?

She also didn't have any other choices, because after she'd maxed out the cash allowance on her cards back at the airport in Boston, she'd ditched her purse, cards and identification and everything, too afraid someone could track her movements.

"The police took me into a private room in the hotel," she said softly. She couldn't look at them, kept her gaze focused on her plate. "I made a phone call to the pal—to my sister." She'd almost blurted out that she'd called the *palace*. How stupid could she be? She was terrible at subterfuge. "There was— something was going on there as well."

The two men seemed to take her meaning without her having to explain everything—at least not for now. Gideon seemed the kind of person who left no secret unexplored. Pushy as he was.

She couldn't exactly say *bomb* aloud without risking someone overhearing and making the connection.

A bomb had been set off at the palace gates, nearly hitting a limousine that carried her younger sister, Mia. Just thinking about it made any remaining appetite vanish. Alessandra pushed her plate slightly away.

Her older sister Eloise had assured her that she and Mia and their father were fine, that most of the staff had been unharmed, but that they were on lockdown.

"I was told to go underground," she whispered. "Without Tim, I...did the best I could."

The visit to New York was only to last a few days, and the palace security team had deemed it completely safe. Tim had been her only guard.

How wrong they'd been.

Matt nodded, eyes sympathetic. She hesitated to turn her head and take in Gideon's expression. When she finally looked, his eyes were narrowed, assessing. Did he think she was *lying*?

"Any idea who wants—who would do something like this?"

She'd followed his first sentence before he'd cut himself off. *Any idea who wants you dead?*

"My aunt."

~ * ~

An hour and a half later, Gideon paced in the farmhouse kitchen, feeling caged.

He wanted to do more than pace. He wanted to put his fist through something.

He couldn't believe he'd agreed to Matt's farfetched plan. *Hide a princess on the Triple H?*

Matt had been right when he'd said they couldn't

leave the princess to her own devices. She'd lucked out when she'd jumped in the back of his truck, finding help instead of someone who would do her harm. It was obvious she had no idea how to survive on her own. She hadn't even taken the time to purchase some cheap, touristy clothes in one of the airport shops, which might've given her some anonymity while she'd traveled. She'd still been wearing the slinky evening dress and heels she'd worn at the time of the shooting!

It would've been easy for Gideon to track her, if that had been his assignment.

He could only hope and pray that whoever had come after her in New York was a moron, or that their assignment had been to scare her off, not kill her.

He wanted answers from her so-called security team. He'd questioned her in-depth in the truck on the ride here, but she'd claimed they'd deemed her trip safe, kept the security light.

There could be someone on the inside. It was possible. That was one explanation for letting as assassin get so close to her.

Or else they were idiots.

He might be one too, because if someone was still after her, he'd just put his own family in danger. And that was something he couldn't live with.

With calving season upon them, he didn't have time to babysit a spoiled, rich princess who undoubtedly was used to a large staff catering to her every whim. He'd already reached out to one of his old SEAL teammates, Cash, asked for information about the investigation behind the shooting and bombing—he'd had to pry that out of her too—and gave him a heads up as to the princess's location. The other man had advised Gideon to lay low, keep her hidden.

This was a huge mistake. Gideon knew it, but he hadn't been able to talk Matt out of it or think of another solution on the fly. And looking down on the princess's wide, frightened eyes, he hadn't been able to tell her *no*, either.

He'd been shocked to feel compassion flare when she'd become visibly upset over the death of her bodyguard. That she'd felt such deep emotion over the loss of someone she employed made her seem...human. Almost.

He heard a tread on the stairs and stopped pacing. Faced the mission head-on, hands at his sides.

Her feet came into view first—bare—as she descended the steps from the second floor. Then a slender pair of legs encased in jeans. They were borrowed from a stash of clothes his sister had left behind and fit a little too snugly in the hips. A chambray work shirt over a faded T-shirt completed the outfit. With her hair pulled back in a braid behind her head, she looked the part of a working cowgirl.

He knew how badly appearances could deceive.

As she landed on the second-to-last step, her gaze lifted and their eyes met. Something in the soft blue depths hit him square in the chest.

It was uncomfortable. And he didn't like it. He flicked his gaze away, instead staring just over her right shoulder.

"You'll want to stay in the house," he said, voice a bit more gruff than he'd intended. "There's livestock roaming every pasture, and you're likely to get stepped on or scare them—and most of them are calving right now."

She nodded slowly.

He went on. "We're having supper tonight to celebrate my brother's leave—time off. You can stay out of sight, if you want. Or you can come down, meet all the hands. And my sister, Carrie."

She pressed her palms together, interlocking her fingers just in front of her midsection. A picture of calm. But he caught the slight tremble of her hands. "Is there anything I can do to help?"

He didn't figure someone who got waited on hand-and-foot knew her way around a kitchen, so the offer sounded pretty weak to him. "Nope. Just lay low."

He needed to get back out to the barn, get Dan on the radio and make sure the boys were making progress fencing off the far south pasture, but there was one more thing.

He approached the princess, bristling internally when she tensed. He knew she must be having a rough time of it, but he'd opened his home to her, offered his protection. Not something he did lightly. The least she could do was not flinch when he came near.

"Here," he gruffed. He held out his smartphone.

She just stared at him.

Finally, impatient, he waggled it. "Take it," he ordered. "It's mine. For emergencies. I've got a burner phone I can use for now. I've programmed numbers for me and Matt at the top of the contacts. I'd hold off calling or emailing your family for now— it's possible a hacker could intercept the signal and track where you are. Possible, not likely," he amended when her face paled.

She took the phone from him, her fingers a cool brush against his palm. "Thank you." She looked him directly, which bought her a modicum of respect. "For everything. I know I'm putting you out, and I hope to give you a more official thank you when I can get back to—to the palace."

He didn't need her thanks, but he nodded anyway. "I've got work to do."

~ * ~

Alessandra stood in the hallway after Gideon the Bear had stalked past her and out through what appeared to be a mudroom, judging by the number of dirty boots piled on a rug next to the back door.

She should really stop thinking of him that way. He might look like a bear, might snarl and snuffle and grunt like one, but he'd shown her kindness by offering his home. Reluctant though the offer might have been.

She turned the phone over in her hands, at a loss.

Normally, every moment of her day was scheduled. Events for charities the palace supported. Keynote speeches. Time spent being updated on current events across the globe. Except for the scant, early-morning hours where she snuck "below-stairs," she rarely had time to herself.

Thus, the loss. She didn't know what to do with herself.

She turned a slow circle, taking in her surroundings. When they'd arrived, Matt had taken a phone call and wandered off toward the big, red barn that was situated on a slight hill above the house.

Gideon had brought her inside and given her the change of clothes, but it was obvious he'd been in a hurry to get back to his work. She'd barely looked around when she'd come inside.

At the foot of the stairs, she stood in what appeared to be the heart of the home. The staircase landed in the center of the house, and all directions led somewhere else. The mudroom and back door were at the end of a short hallway, directly behind where she stood. Another offshoot led to—she peeked through a swinging door—the kitchen. She normally wasn't so nosy, but Gideon hadn't told her she couldn't look around.

She raised on the balls of her bare feet for long seconds before she committed herself. Then started off.

The kitchen was a mess. Someone had make breakfast, but the remains of eggs stuck in a pan on the stovetop, now brown. A biscuit pan was empty of bread, but had rings of cooked-on residue where it hadn't been scraped. A pile of plates sat next to the sink.

The countertops were littered with old mail, other assorted dishes and a...she didn't know what kind of farm implement it was, but the pronged tool looked dangerous. And like it belonged in the barn, not the kitchen. The cabinets were dated, the stain almost worn off in some places. The wallpaper was faded, and the fridge an old model.

The entire room was in need of an update and a thorough cleaning. Matt had said Gideon ran the ranch with several "hands"—cowboys, she thought. Did the mess really not bother the group of bachelors?

She wandered through the room and into a dining room. Only it was like no dining room she'd seen before. A rough-hewn wooden picnic table took up the center of the room. It would've been country charming if there had been any decoration to go with it. The table was bare, walls were bare, even the hardwood floor could've used a rug. And a good scrubbing.

Well, it was...functional. Certainly big enough to seat ten or so men. Maybe eight, if they were all as large as Gideon.

She edged past the table and back through the entryway she'd passed through earlier. This time, she kept going instead of turning back to the center staircase.

The family room had a lived-in look. The two low couches bookended a coffee table that had so many water rings that it almost seemed planned. A flat-screen TV took up one wall, and opposite that, a large rock fireplace appeared inviting. But there was no throw over the back of the couch, no homey touches anywhere.

She wandered through the entryway and past the staircase to the back corner of the house, the only place she hadn't explored. There were three doorways off the hall here. Bathroom. Linen closet. Bedroom.

She stood in the doorway, frozen for a long moment. The bed was made, a simple quilt thrown across it as bedspread. Curtains framed the window looking out on blue sky. A dresser was cluttered with a collection of spare change and, in the back corner, a huge, gold belt buckle.

On the side table stood two pictures. One was Matt, a woman that must be his sister, and... could that clean-shaven man be Gideon?

He was handsome. With his chiseled jaw and those sharp eyes, laugh lines fanning from his eyes... he would have caught her eye if they'd met in different circumstances.

Was this Gideon's room?

In the picture, a gray-haired man stood behind the three, his arms stretched to encompass them. Their father?

Behind the picture was another. She'd stepped into the room before she really meant to. Close enough to see the photo.

It was a candid shot of several men in camouflage sitting around in the desert. They were heavily armed with scary-looking black guns in hand. In this one, Gideon sported a shorter, trimmed beard and dark sunglasses.

He was laughing.

Something tugged deep in the pit of her stomach. A response to the man, even though he wasn't here.

She shouldn't be in his room. She backed up even as she realized she'd intruded into his personal domain.

She wouldn't like it if he'd invaded the inner sanctuary of her rooms back at the palace. He'd probably hate knowing she was in here.

She quickly ducked out of the room and regrouped in the hallway, wrapping her arms around her middle.

What had happened to that smiling soldier? What had turned him into a surly grizzly bear?

Her thoughts dissipated.

Even though she stood in a patch of sunlight slanting in from the large picture windows in the living room, she didn't feel warm.

She was here, on a ranch in the middle of nowhere, Texas. She was safe.

But there was a part of her, a big part, that was also lost.

CHAPTER FOUR

If Alessandra had expected Gideon to be the worst-groomed of the cowhands, she would've been sorely disappointed that evening.

After the past, crazy forty-odd hours, she'd hit a wall sometime in the early afternoon. She'd dragged herself upstairs to lie down on the bed and only wakened when the noise level in the house below rose loud enough that it shook the rafters.

She was still mulling over Gideon's hesitant invitation. Should she go downstairs and join the party?

There was a small mirror on the tall chest of drawers next to the twin bed in the room she'd been given, and she squinted at her reflection in the fading light filtering through the curtains. Squinted her eyes more tightly together, so she wouldn't have to see the rat's nest that was her hair. The braid she'd put in earlier had come halfway apart, and one side of her hair stuck up in a matted mess where she'd slept on

53

it.

This was one time she wouldn't have minded having her stylist on hand. She'd never had to worry about getting her hair right, because Anna was there to help her.

She untangled the rest of the braid and picked up the brush that Gideon had found for her somewhere. It pulled her hair when she began the first strokes. She'd showered earlier, and the conditioner was a cheap brand that made her hair feel rough between her fingers.

She didn't even have her own toiletries.

She stifled the whine that wanted to escape and set about brushing her hair and then pulling it into a tight French braid that hopefully wouldn't look as messy as she felt inside.

A quick stop in the bathroom to splash her face and pinch her cheeks—neither did she have any makeup—and she forced herself to the head of the stairs.

Her stomach rumbled, making the decision for her.

Plus, there was no use hiding up here. She had a hunch Matt would come looking for her, even if the irascible Gideon wouldn't.

Downstairs, it was even louder. Men's voices and raucous laughter rang out through the house. The swinging door to the kitchen was closed, but she could hear the clanging of dishes and the movement of what might have been two people in there.

Most of the noise was coming from the living room.

She hesitated in the shadowed hall, looking in.

Gideon was closest to her, on the other side of the large open archway. He stood with feet slightly apart and arms crossed, what might be a scowl under his beard.

On the far couch, two men she didn't recognize lounged negligently, their dusty boots stretched out in front of them. She winced, thinking about the floor. One still wore a cowboy hat and let his head loll back on the couch. Both of them looked as if they'd been in their faded, dirty clothes for days. And both sported long, unkempt beards, like Gideon wore. Was this a Texas thing? Or a ranch hand thing? Did no one wash up for supper?

Matt perched on a barstool across the room, talking animatedly with another man, this one with a shock of short-cropped red hair. She couldn't see his face.

She must've moved, or maybe Gideon just sensed her presence, because his head turned toward her before she was ready to be spotted.

He cleared his throat and the room quieted

instantly, everyone's attention on him.

"Guys, this is the little gal I was telling you about. Meet Allie."

She stepped into the light as three pairs of eyes— plus Matt's glinting gaze—swiveled toward her.

She'd keynoted enough that she was used to being the center of attention. Used to being in the spotlight, having cameras pointed at her. But this...she felt their attention acutely.

"Nate and Trey there on the couch," Gideon said with a nod.

She tried to smile, but it felt tremulous.

"And Brian," he motioned to the redhead near Matt. "Chase and Dan are putting the finishing touches on supper."

Often at public events, she had an aide nearby at all times to whisper a name in her ear or prompt her into conversation before she could make a mistake.

She floundered now.

"Thank you for opening your home to me," she said softly.

"It's Gideon's place," either Trey or Nate said from the couch with a big grin. "Interesting that he brought you out here. He usually keeps his distance from any pretty woman."

Trey-slash-Nate cut him off with an elbow to the ribs, eliciting a huff of air from the other man.

Gideon growled.

"It's my place too," Matt said easily, diverting attention from his brother.

"For now." Gideon said. "Not sure how long me'n Carrie will let you keep your shares, since you're pretty much career military."

She let her gaze slide to Gideon. Had he helped Matt avert the conversation from her purposely?

"He's never liked shoveling—" Brian started to say something crude but caught himself halfway through the word with a glance at Alessandra. Splotches of red climbed in his cheeks—he was clean shaven. "Sorry, ma'am."

She let it go with a shrug and a smile. She had no intention of coming in here and asking these men to change their lifestyles to suit her. They were doing *her* a favor.

But a glance at Gideon showed his face looked like a thundercloud.

Then someone knocked on the door. Matt jumped up from his stool.

She moved out of the way as Matt came toward her, heading for the door. He didn't quite get it open.

"Uncle Matt!"

The exuberant cry preceded a tornado of a small brunette girl who launched herself through the doorway at her uncle. Matt swept her up easily into his arms. A woman who must be Carrie, Gideon and Matt's sister, stepped over the threshold, and she too threw herself at Matt. He caught her too.

Alessandra caught the small sob that escaped the woman, even though her face was buried in Matt's shoulder.

Alessandra was intruding.

Her gaze connected with Gideon's where he stood opposite, behind the cluster of his family.

If she wasn't mistaken, his eyes had a sheen of moisture too.

~ * ~

Gideon was intensely aware of Alessandra at the dinner table, two seats away with his niece Scarlett between them.

Part of him really wanted to know what the princess thought of their gathering. This must be a lot different than what she was used to. The hands were in fine form, boisterous and loud as they showed off for both women. The one-course meal of hearty spaghetti and meatballs, salad and crusty garlic bread, was probably much simpler fare than she was used to. Their cutlery could never be called *silver*ware. And Apollo made a practice of crawling on the floor beneath the table, licking up any crumb that dared be dropped.

Although Scarlett had clung to Matt for a good ten minutes when his sister had arrived, she'd elected to sit next to Gideon at the supper table, and somehow wrangled Alessandra into the chair on her other side. With the shortie between them, he kept catching glances, finding himself in the laser sight of Alessandra's bright smile.

Although she was definitely out of place—quiet and unassuming—he caught the tail end of several of her smiles in response to something the guys or Scarlett had said. She was fresh, like a spring tulip. The diamond in a room full of coal lumps.

Once, when she'd laughed at something dumb Nate had said, Gideon had gotten a bite of meatball lodged in his esophagus. It stayed there, a hard lump that had him shifting uncomfortably in his seat.

He felt old. Out of place. Grumpy. Just like Matt had said earlier.

His brother was quieter than usual. Gideon still believed something had happened during his tour. Gideon had had one or two near-fatal incidents, and when you came home after something like that...well, it changed how you looked at things. How you treated the people you cared about.

He just wished his little brother hadn't had to go through it.

"Uncle Gid," Scarlett piped, distracting him from his thoughts.

"Yeah, squirt?" He never got tired of looking at the little upturned face.

Scarlett was four going on twenty-five, and he was a sucker for the freckles splashed across the bridge of her pert nose and those big, cornflower blue eyes.

Scarlett scooted close, her little shoulder brushing his elbow. She motioned for him to lean down. So he did, aware of Alessandra's attention on the two of them.

"I think Allie is a princess." Scarlett's breath was warm and smelled of garlic, and it distracted him long enough that he had to play her words over a second time before he grasped their meaning.

His stomach somersaulted. If his four-year-old niece could recognize Alessandra, they were in for a world of trouble. Had Carrie been playing the national news channel at home?

"What makes you think that, squirt?" Somehow he managed to get the words out evenly.

"Look how long her hair is," the pipsqueak whispered, her head bumping his chin as she turned to shoot a look at their guest and then quickly turned back when Alessandra caught her looking. "I think she's Rapunzel."

Reality intruded as his eyes focused on the long

braid that hung down Alessandra's back and past her waist. Rapunzel, indeed.

"I don't know, squirt," he said softly. "She looks kinda regular to me."

Not really. Even wearing clothes that were similar to every one else's at the table, there was a different air to Alessandra. It wasn't entirely her posture—although she sat straighter than anyone he'd ever met, as if she balanced a book on her head at all times—and she hadn't tilted her nose up once. It was something else. Just *her*, maybe. She was too fine.

Whatever it was, she didn't belong here.

Tired of waiting on him or maybe dissatisfied with his answer, Scarlett turned to the princess. "Are you Rapunzel?"

"No, I'm not," Alessandra answered. "Is she your favorite princess?"

Scarlett shrugged. "I like the ice princess and her sister."

He didn't figure she was up on the latest animated princess movies, but Alessandra leaned closer to Scarlett. "Oh, I like her too. But really, the reindeer is my favorite character from that movie. Do you know the song he sings?"

She hummed a few bars until Scarlett belted out some words that sounded like gibberish to him, then both females dissolved into giggles.

Someone kicked his foot from beneath the table. He glared across to see his sister, squished in between Matt and Brian, watching him speculatively.

His ranch hands weren't as subtle.

"Boss, you planning on needing some time off?" Dan asked from the other end of the table. "Maybe doing some courting?"

Guffaws went around the room.

Fire flared in his cheeks, but hopefully the beard camouflaged it. Scarlett was chattering to the princess, so maybe they'd missed the joke at his expense.

He wasn't sitting here mooning over the girl. He was listening in to make sure she didn't slip up and put his family in danger. Protecting Scarlett.

That was it.

If he did feel a bolt of attraction, he would never have an opportunity to act on it. Right. Imagine someone like *her* taking up with him. They'd rub each other the wrong way. What about him attending a palace function? They'd probably want to sprinkle glitter in his beard.

But an uncomfortable clutch of his chest remained.

~ * ~

The group sat around the table, talking, for a long time after supper. Scarlett relocated to Matt's knee, regaling her uncle of tales about her preschool friends while Matt listened attentively. Gideon would have to get to the bottom of what was bugging his brother eventually.

Scarlett's desertion left a space between him and the princess, and he noticed Alessandra disappear from the table before too long. She'd probably gone upstairs to sleep. Or relax. Or whatever. Was probably bored with their simple talk of ranching and the folks in town. It was for the best, anyway. She'd be here a few days, maybe, then go back to her ritzy life.

The hands had accepted his explanation of a damsel in trouble without asking for a lot of details— but apparently they wanted to believe she was more to him than a mere acquaintance.

Ha.

When he carried his plate from the table into the kitchen, he found her elbow-deep in a sink full of sudsy water, scrubbing pots. Apollo lay at her feet, his black nose resting on brown paws.

Seeing her like this made that uncomfortable pinch in his chest return full bore.

Of all the things he'd imagined her doing, the dishes wasn't one of them. Had the noise of their conversations completed drowned out the clanking of pots and pans, the swish of the water?

"Everything okay?" he asked.

She startled and looked over her shoulder at him, their gazes connecting again. He easily read the shadows in her eyes.

"I'm fine." The firm set of her lips might indicate otherwise.

He wasn't going to push her, not now.

"We're kind of a rowdy bunch," he said. Not really apologizing. And stating the obvious.

She *hmmed*, but didn't agree or disagree.

"Sort of an acquired taste. Like black coffee. Or sushi."

This time, he won a small smile, seen only because she'd turned her head slightly toward him. He didn't know why it mattered, but seeing it made the tight knot in his chest loosen up, just slightly.

"Don't blame you at all for needing to take us in small doses."

She smiled again, just a small twitch of her mouth, but shook her head. Agreeing that his hands and his family were best a teaspoon at time? Or was she disagreeing?

She didn't explain.

"Nobody expects you to clean up after us, you know." He deposited his dirty plate and fork on the counter near her. It was conspicuously clean, as if it'd been freshly scrubbed—and the counter along the opposite side of the sink was laid out with clean dishes drying on towels. She'd been busy.

He moved to her other side. He picked up the last towel on the line she'd laid out and started drying the nearest item, the scrambled eggs skillet from this morning. It was spotless. He well knew how the egg residue cemented to the pan when it was left all day. And that was only one of the dishes that had littered the kitchen.

It even smelled cleaner in here. Like lemons.

He might've thought that Brian—on dinner duty—had cleaned up, if he didn't know his men so well. They preferred to leave the mess until there were no more dishes to use before anyone would take initiative.

"Inspecting my work?" she asked. Her attention remained on the pot she was vigorously scrubbing. He winced. Was it from yesterday? Or two days ago?

"No..."

But she must've heard the weak denial in his tone, because she frowned as she scrubbed even harder. "Maybe you think a pr—" She glanced over her shoulder. So did he. They were alone. "A person like me wouldn't know how to wash dishes."

That was exactly what he'd thought. Didn't being

born a princess mean she'd grown up with a silver spoon in her mouth?

~ * ~

It shouldn't bother Alessandra that Gideon thought she was unable to perform a simple task, such as doing dishes. It wasn't exactly a skill she was known for.

She used the dishrag to scrub at one particular caked-on bit of gunk in the bottom corner of the pan. "When I was fourteen..." Soon after her father had started to seriously decline. "I started sneaking down to the kitchens in the wee hours of the morning. Our on-staff chef put me to work. Baking bread, helping with breakfast...and other things. He believed that anyone working in his kitchen should know how to clean up after themselves. Even me."

Chef Marco had become like a beloved uncle to her, though he was paid staff. Even as a teen, she'd known better than to air the family's private business to anyone. So even though she'd never talked about the overwhelming grief of watching her father decline, Marco had known. Had provided a steady presence, even as he put on a gruff outward act of not wanting the princess in his domain.

Marco and Krissy and Bella, two of the

housemaids, had been more of a family to her than anyone else, but as her responsibilities to represent Glorvaird grew, she'd grown more distant from them.

Thinking about her sort-of-staff, sort-of-friends was why she'd eventually had to leave the group of boisterous cowboys and Carrie and Scarlett. She missed the familiar. Missed home.

More than anything, she'd wanted a family like this one. Oh, they didn't all have DNA ties, but it was clear that the cowhands had an affection for each other, even through the ribbing and teasing. It was also clear they respected Gideon and his leadership as he ran the place.

Her own family...well, her father and older sister were difficult. And Mia, her younger sister, was often gone, flitting around social events.

He hadn't responded to her story about helping in the kitchen, and she glanced at him to see his brow furrowed above the flat cookie tray he was drying.

She nudged his elbow with hers and tried for a smile. "It isn't as if I haven't made judgments about you, too."

She couldn't pinpoint what exactly made her spout the teasing statement. There was safety in being reserved, holding herself separate from someone she would likely only know for a matter of days. But something inside her wanted to erase the deep grooves in his forehead.

"What do you mean?"

"Just that." She was unable to prevent her lips from twitching with a smile at his frown.

She motioned to his face. "I spent the entire morning thinking of you as *Gideon the Bear*, because of how you go around growling and grunting at everyone. And, well...you seem sort of dangerous..." She trailed off. She'd meant to say something about his dark, overgrown beard and hair that needed a trim, even motioned in a halfhearted circle toward his head. She'd meant to make him smile. It hadn't worked.

His frown didn't lift. It deepened. Her stomach pitched.

"But," she continued quickly, "when you're with your niece, you're more of a teddy bear." She'd been shocked at first, to see him smiling with Scarlett, who obviously had him wrapped around her little finger.

She'd even heard him chuckle once. Seen the flash of white teeth behind his beard. His eyes had *sparkled*.

Those moments had been like looking at a totally different man. An attractive one, like the picture she'd stumbled upon in his bedroom.

"So my initial assessment was wrong," she said quickly, before her thoughts could get—more—out of control. "Or at least, not completely correct. You have a tough side that was probably necessary as an active-duty soldier. And you also have a...sweet side."

She snapped her mouth shut, realizing she was babbling. And blundering. She'd nearly scrubbed the finish off the pot and quickly moved to rinse it in the second sink.

There was no avoiding Gideon as she upended the damp pot on one of the drying towels. He set aside the towel and leaned one hip against the countertop. Crossed his arms over his chest.

Her face burned. She certainly hadn't meant to say so much. There was something about him that made her nervous.

She barely dared to look up into his eyes, afraid she'd offended him in some way. When she did, she couldn't read his expression. His eyes glittered slightly, but the masked emotion could be anger or humor or anything, really.

Finally, he spoke. "So you're saying you're a"—his eyes widened slightly—"*you-know-what*, who likes to do dishes."

His nostrils flared slightly, and one corner of his mouth tipped up. He was teasing her?

Movement from behind them broke the moment, and she flushed, quickly going back to the sink, though the mountain of dirty dishes had been reduced to a more manageable hill.

"Gideon, are you picking on your houseguest?" It was Carrie's strident voice. "You don't have to clean up after these pigs—I mean bachelors—honey."

The other woman touched Alessandra's shoulder, a gesture meant to convey solidarity, but the unexpected touch startled her. People usually weren't so familiar. Of course, Carrie didn't know her true identity either, or she might not get so close.

Alessandra hated the subterfuge, though she understood why it was necessary.

Gideon backed away, raising both hands in front of himself. "I didn't make her do anything. I walked in, and she was already halfway through the pile."

Carrie moved into the place beside Alessandra that he'd recently vacated, picking up the damp towel and twisting it into some kind of snapping weapon that she wielded to drive him out of the room. She joined Alessandra beside the sink and took up the task of drying, much more efficiently than Gideon had.

"I don't know what kind of trouble you're in," Carrie said, voice low, "and I don't need to know. Gideon and his boys will take care of you."

Alessandra didn't know whether the woman was gearing up for a warning, but she braced herself anyway.

"I just wanted you to know that if you need a

woman to talk to, I'm not too far away. My place in town is only about a ten-minute drive from here. I work afternoons, while Scarlett is in school."

The offer was so unexpected that tears welled in Alessandra's eyes. She blinked them back. "Thank you."

"I'm planning on making a run out here in the morning, after I drop Scarlett at class. I doubt either of my brothers thought to provide you anything more than a bar of rough soap and a change of clothes. I've got some things you can borrow, and I'll stop by the drug store for the essentials."

Carrie's words were so true that Alessandra couldn't help the wet giggle that emerged. "Thank you. Very much."

Carrie shook her head in an exaggerated manner. "We grew up together, but I don't think I rubbed off on them all that much. They don't know an eyelash curler from a flat iron, and heaven forbid you start crying in front of them. Easiest way to get rid of them in a pinch, by the way. Of course, Mom was gone by the time we were teenagers."

Alessandra handed Carrie the next dish. They were down to the supper plates now, the water in the sink grown tepid. "My mother died when I was five."

They shared a glance. It was a unifying thing. Losing a mother was something you never quite got over.

They finished the rest of the dishes in no time at all, Gideon's sister carrying the conversation, mostly talking about Scarlett. There was no mention of Scarlett's father, and Alessandra couldn't help wondering what had happened to him, though she didn't get up the guts to ask.

They wiped off their hands on clean towels. Alessandra's were pruny from being in the water so long. Carrie kept her eyes down. "About Gideon... He's got a good heart, but...he won't open up. Don't expect too much from him."

Carrie raised her head, her eyes trying to impart the message that Alessandra was struggling to comprehend. "I-I won't," she said, because that's what Carrie seemed to expect.

Did everyone thing she and Gideon were involved? She remembered his earlier statement at the diner that he hadn't dated in a long while. Were his friends and family just seeing what they wanted to see?

Was there any use in telling the other woman that she had absolutely no expectations of Gideon? He'd offered her sanctuary while the royal security force worked with the Glorvaird and New York law enforcement teams to investigate the shooting and bombing. When the head of palace security was able to find her a secure way home, she'd return to the family duty that awaited her.

Carrie surprised her with a goodbye hug. Alessandra had to fight not to tighten up at the familiarity.

It made her nose sting.

When was the last time one of her own sisters had hugged her?

She couldn't remember.

LACY WILLIAMS

CHAPTER FIVE

That same night, Gideon stayed late in the birthing barn. He watched a mama giving birth, just making sure everything went the way it was supposed to.

He was afraid to go back to the house. Afraid that, even though it was late, he would run into Alessandra again. That she'd start rambling in that adorable way that made him want to smile. Or hug her.

Gideon the Bear.

There was a little jagged piece of broken mirror nailed to one of the studs on the far wall, and he caught a bit of his scowling reflection.

The Bear.

It wasn't the worst thing he'd been called in his life.

He tilted his head slightly, catching sight of the unkempt hair and scraggly beard. He looked like a mountain man. A little like a real bear.

He jerked his chin up, and there was that scowl again in the reflection.

He didn't really growl and grunt all the time, did he? He ran his hand through his beard, a little ashamed of himself. Since when did he not care?

Sure, he had high expectations. He paid his hands better than any other ranch around, and if they slacked off on the job, it ticked him off. The Triple H ran a large herd and every cog had to operate.

And when someone hitched an unexpected ride in his truck, something that could potentially put his family in danger, he might've come off a little grumpy...

Was that really how she saw him? How everybody saw him? She'd seemed to admire his interaction with Scarlett, but the rest hadn't been very complimentary.

And she'd been right. He'd judged her harshly, thinking she didn't have any experience with domestic chores.

He didn't know what to think about her story about hanging out in the kitchens with the royal chef. There had been a slight pause when she'd begun the story. One that made him think there was more behind the story than she'd told him.

Or was that just his suspicious, grizzly-like nature, rearing its head?

There was a computer in the tack room, in the area of the barn closed off to protect it from the elements. It was an old one, but it had Internet access.

He took one last look at the cow and decided she could work on her own for awhile before he pushed through the door toward the tack room.

It took longer than he would've liked for the old machine to boot up, but within a few minutes he was logged on to the Internet, searching for everything he could find about her family. Something he probably should've done earlier in the day, and would've if he hadn't lost time bringing the princess out here and then checking in with all the hands.

Her mom had passed away when she was little. He felt a sympathetic pang, because it was something they had in common. There were some old mentions of concerns over the King's health, but they seemed to taper off after a few years.

The crown princess, Alessandra's older sister, had been in a car accident as a preteen and bore scars across her face and torso. She had been basically out of public sight, no pictures or anything, until her coronation when she came of age at eighteen. He'd seen worse. She would never be a grand beauty, but he didn't think the scars detracted that much from her looks. The gossip rags, however, claimed she had a beastly personality. He couldn't find one picture of her smiling, and sure enough, in several paparazzi shots, she wore a nasty snarl across her face.

Alessandra's younger sister seemed to be in the media all the time. Her bubbly smile came through in pixels, and he could guess she enjoyed the attention. She was young but seemed to be on the arm of several handsome young men at different times. A social butterfly? Or did she enjoy toying with young men's affections? It was impossible to know.

Alessandra didn't get as much media coverage as either of her sisters. She appeared regularly at charity events and palace-sponsored occasions. Her smile was much more reserved than her younger sister's. After interacting with her today, he didn't think what he was studying on his screen was her real smile at all.

At breakfast, she'd claimed her aunt might be behind the bombing and assassination attempt. He searched for information on a possible family feud but didn't find much. The king's sister had been estranged since her eighteenth birthday. She'd married and had two sons, now about the same age as Alessandra and her sisters. The reason for the estrangement wasn't publicized. Nothing was mentioned anywhere about the aunt's relationship to the crown being revoked. Which meant the king's nephews were technically princes in their own right.

What could make a woman hate the king and his daughters so much that she tried to kill them?

It wasn't his job to find out. It wasn't even really his job to protect Alessandra, but he'd taken it on. He'd give Cash a couple of days for reconnaissance, and hopefully things would settle down enough for her to go home.

He couldn't wait for things to get back to normal.

~ * ~

Alessandra couldn't sleep.

She'd gone to bed, even dozed a little, but nightmares quickly followed. Of those awful moments when Tim had surged toward her in the crowd. The muted *pop!* of the gun discharging. And Tim's blood after he'd knocked her to the ground.

Then the scene went a little fuzzy.

Her dream-self pressed harder on Tim's chest, trying to save him. Only something had changed. She looked closely at his face and realized her dream self was pressing on *Gideon's* chest. That it was *Gideon's* broken body beneath her hands.

She woke with a gasp.

She bolted up in the twin bed, breathed deeply.

The bed was safe. Lumpier than anything she was used to, but safe. She tucked the quilt over her knees and wrapped her arms around herself.

She couldn't deal with whatever part of her

subconscious had put Gideon into the dream. Surely it was because he'd been kind to her, and he'd been one of the last people she'd seen before she'd gone to bed. And he was protecting her.

That was all there was to it, right?

She grieved for Tim, tears falling now as she thought about the man who'd given his life for her. Who would comfort his sister and mother back in Glorvaird?

Until now, she hadn't paid attention to the other thoughts that she'd shoved away after Tim's death. But questions swirled now. How had a killer gotten so close to her? Close enough that her bodyguard had barely had time to step into the line of fire? Although some events she attended were publicized on the palace website and in the media, her exact schedule was never confirmed. Tim had been her only bodyguard, but there was a team of hired men and women who scouted each location, each function she attended beforehand. And everyone in that crowd was supposed to have been invited to the party.

She didn't have answers.

She also didn't think her aunt—if that's who'd initiated the bombing and the shooting—would give up. She didn't know the woman personally, and Father didn't talk about her much, but there were always whispers among the staff about her aunt's unhappiness with the way her father ruled the country. Helena wanted to rule.

But because of the bloodlines, she would have to kill all of them—the king and his three daughters—before she would be crowned. Would the people of Glorvaird even accept her if she was behind the killings? Perhaps that's why it was so hard to connect the attempted killings to anyone. Her aunt was covering her tracks, and well.

Or perhaps it hadn't been her aunt after all, though Alessandra couldn't think of another party with such violent intentions toward her family. Glorvaird was a small, peaceful country that relied on trade with its neighbors and worked to keep peaceful agreements in place.

Knowing her swirling thoughts weren't conducive to sleep, Alessandra got out of bed. The bedroom was bare and simple, with not even a television to distract her.

Because she had only the clothes that Gideon had given her, she'd gone to bed in just a T-shirt and undergarments. Now she pulled the jeans back on. Then she slipped into the hallway.

She paused on the top step, one hand covering the smile that bloomed. She hadn't heard it from inside her room, but heavy snores emanated from most of the upstairs bedrooms. She knew the ranch hands worked hard. Guessed they played hard. Apparently, they slept hard, too.

She crept downstairs, but there was no sign of anyone else awake. The microwave clock in the kitchen read one a.m. and she guessed the crew had to be out working early.

But knowing that didn't get her any closer to a restful state. She needed something to *do*.

And she found it in the kitchen.

She'd finished the dishes earlier, but Carrie had shooed her out before she'd attacked any of the other cleaning issues. Not that she hadn't noticed and catalogued them.

The countertops and window needed a good washing. As did the microwave, stovetop, and oven. Even the shelves in the cabinets wore a layer of dust between where the dishes rested.

And the floor was desperately in need of a good mopping.

She turned on the soft light over the sink, not the full overhead light, hoping that she wouldn't wake Gideon in his back bedroom. She found a plethora of cleaning supplies beneath the sink. Mostly unopened.

And she set to work.

~ * ~

Gideon had slept hard after foolishly being out in the barn so late—for the second night in a row. He woke abruptly.

Something was wrong.

Light streamed through his window, which meant he'd overslept by at least an hour and a half. The clock read seven-thirty.

The hands were going to give him heck for sleeping in.

He emerged from his room minutes later, running one hand through his hair. And stopped cold.

Someone had baked. The sweet smell of cinnamon and sugar wafted through the house.

He found Dan and Trey standing in the foyer, a plate in each of their hands, shoveling food into their mouths. Judging from the crumbs on their plates, they'd enjoyed...were those cinnamon rolls? And some kind of pie made from eggs and vegetables. They were staring into the living room until he approached, and then Dan started to swivel away, defending the remaining eggs on his plate.

"What's going on?" Gideon asked.

"Shh," Trey shushed him with a scandalized look into the living room.

Gideon frowned and stepped forward so he could

see.

Alessandra was curled up on the far couch. Sleeping. One hand was tucked beneath her face. Her hair was loose and wavy—probably from the braid she'd worn yesterday—and formed a cloud all around her.

Why wasn't she upstairs, in her own bed?

"She must've made breakfast," Dan murmured from behind him. "Sticky buns and quiche in the oven when I got up."

"Cleaned the whole kitchen too," Trey whispered.

Gideon hadn't been able to tear his gaze from the sleeping princess, but now he registered the spray bottle and dirty rag on the low table not far from where she lay.

He sniffed again, this time registering the scent of lemony soap beneath the food smells. *She'd cleaned?*

Sure enough, his boots didn't stick to the kitchen floor when he finally turned them that direction. The appliances were *shiny*. Even the sunlight seemed to sparkle through the window. Everything was spotless.

"Cleaning fairy got us in here, too," Matt called out from the dining room.

Gideon bypassed the tray of buns and the dish with eggs that sat on the stovetop—for now—to stick his head through the doorway. Matt, Nate,

Brian and Chase all lounged around the table, stuffing their faces. The dog was under the table again.

"Why are you all not at work already?"

"Breakfast," Brian slurred, his mouth full. A piece of eggs zoomed out of his overly full mouth and landed on the table.

Gideon winced. "Do you think someone who spent the night cleaning up after you lot wants to do it all over again? Have a little respect."

Brian looked appropriately abashed and used his fingers to scoop the egg back onto his plate.

"You're gonna keep her around, aren't you?" Chase asked hopefully.

"Yeah," Nate chimed in. "She's a mighty good cook."

Brian swallowed the rest of his food. "Not sure what she sees in you, but you've got to turn on some kind of charm and keep her around."

"Yeah," chimed Trey, as he and Dan joined the crowd from the doorway off the front hall.

Matt's eyes glittered as he looked to Gideon, waiting for the answer like everyone else. Matt should know better than to wear that expression. The woman was a *princess*.

There was no way she could stay, but Gideon couldn't tell the boys that.

He sighed. "I told you yesterday, she's in trouble. Just needs a place to lay low for a few days." But he couldn't resist teasing them. "Besides, do you really think someone like her"—he jerked his finger over his shoulder—"would want to hang around a bunch of hands who think personal grooming is optional and don't even know how to clean up after themselves?"

Matt grinned, shoving another forkful of food into his mouth. The other hands looked down at themselves. They were a rough bunch. Other than Carrie, they didn't interact much with women. Didn't spend much time in town. There wasn't much need to trim a beard or get a haircut. Or buy new clothes.

Like he was one to talk, anyway. She'd called him *Gideon the Bear*. Not just for his personality.

It wasn't as if it mattered anyway, because she'd be leaving soon. They'd go back to their regular routines, and she'd go back to her palace. She wouldn't be around to appreciate it if they all up and decided to shave and wear clean clothes anyway.

But the thought remained lodged in his gut, a boulder.

Matt stood and headed toward the kitchen. Gideon followed, leaving the other hands muttering around the kitchen table.

"Thought I'd saddle up Rufus and do some fence

line checking," Matt said as he moved to wash his plate and cup in the sink. Gideon was glad to see that his brother, at least, wouldn't leave more of a mess for Alessandra. "It's been awhile since I've had a good ride."

Gideon nodded slowly, mentally running over the list of things he'd planned to do today. He made a snap decision. "I'll ride with you. We can catch up. Scarlett and Carrie weren't the only ones who missed you, you know."

It would give him a chance to talk to Matt, see if he could figure out what was causing the shadows in his brother's eyes.

Two hours later, Gideon was enjoying the familiar feel of the horse beneath him and the sounds of the horses whickering to each other.

Even though sometimes he ached to be back with the Teams, this land was part of him.

But a chill wind blew through his coat, and he hadn't gotten any closer to answers about what was going on with Matt. He'd asked about his brother's tour and gotten deflected. Asked if Matt had any romantic prospects, wondering if maybe his brother was having woman problems, and gotten shut down. There was maybe something there, but his brother wasn't talking.

They had been close in high school, before

Gideon had left for the Navy. But that didn't necessarily mean they'd shared each other's confidences. Gideon had stood up for Matt once in a fistfight. Matt had covered for him when a prank had gone wrong.

But they didn't talk about their feelings. They were guys. They just didn't.

Which made it hard now to figure out how to help.

Gideon was left with a nagging feeling that something had happened on tour. But if Matt didn't want to talk about it, how could he get it out of him?

He was on the verge of giving up when he spotted a flash of white against a dark patch of mud, several yards away. He wheeled his horse closer.

Was that a cigarette butt? None of the hands smoked.

He hopped off the horse, bending to examine it. Picked it up. It *was* a butt.

He showed it to Matt, who didn't seem upset about it. "Could've been from someone who snuck on the place to visit the fishing pond."

"Or from someone scouting the place." Gideon didn't like the feel of it. Out of place. On the heels of the princess's arrival.

"Listen, Nate came to me last night, while you were in the barn."

Gideon looked up, still not convinced about the butt, but he flicked it back on the ground.

"He said you're treating him like a hand, not the foreman. You trying to edge him out of his job?"

"*What?*" *Bear.* How long would Alessandra's nickname haunt him?

"You've got to give a man room to do his job," Matt said.

"He's got plenty of room to do it, long as he and the hands get it right."

"You sure that's how he feels?"

Gideon didn't know. He did know he was frustrated at not knowing whether the cigarette butt was something to be worried about. Now this.

He wasn't a micro-manager, not really. Was that how the hands saw him?

He didn't know how much mental energy he could give to this, with a princess to watch out for. It was just one more thing for him to add to his never-ending list.

LACY WILLIAMS

CHAPTER SIX

Around lunchtime, Gideon got a call from Cash that there was some chatter about continuing plots against the Glorvaird royalty.

Which was exactly what he didn't want to hear.

According to Cash, there were no whispers of the princess's location, but after finding the cigarette butt that shouldn't have been there, he spent the afternoon scouting for any other signs that a stranger had been on the ranch.

Hours of riding and tracking didn't turn up anything else, but he couldn't get rid of the sense that someone with an agenda had been here. He'd learned to trust his gut, and his gut was hardly ever wrong.

He spent the next hour in the barn, making calls to locals, asking if they'd seen any suspicious activity. Probably they all thought he was nuts, but he couldn't help that.

The sun was setting and his stomach was growling when he headed across the yard for the house. He hated the feeling of blindness. Hated thinking someone could be watching the place, and he wouldn't know until it was too late.

As he crossed the yard, the back door opened, and the princess appeared, stepping out onto the back porch. Out in the open.

The hair on the back of his neck rose all at once, and he took the porch steps at a run. "Get back," he ordered, but either she didn't share his sense of urgency or she didn't realize anything was wrong, because instead of moving, she froze.

Which meant that he collided with her, full body, knocking her off her feet. He heard her gasp as he swept her along with him, quickly thumping her back against the clapboard siding. It wasn't enough to keep her out of sight, so he tucked her head into his shoulder, too.

"I told you to stay inside," he said harshly, breath sawing in and out of his chest. Adrenaline pulsed through his veins with every throb of his heart.

She said something, but it was muffled against his chest, and he couldn't make it out.

He shuffled the both of them two feet to the left and yanked open the screen door before he pushed her inside, careful to keep himself between her and any possible threat.

Only when he had slammed the interior door shut

and bodily pushed her several feet into the mudroom did he take a deep breath.

"What's the matter? Gideon?" That was Carrie's voice, coming from the kitchen.

Alessandra watched him with eyes wide and dark with fear. All the color had leached from her face.

"Gideon, let go of her."

He still held both of the princess's shoulders, though now she was at arms' length and not pressed close to him. Her flowery scent was burned into his nostrils, into his brain.

"Gideon," Carrie said again.

He shook himself out of the moment, dropped his hands to his sides, realizing for the first time with some clarity that Alessandra was dressed up. Oh, not dressed up, per se, but differently than she had been yesterday. She wore some kind of fuzzy sweater over a pale yellow dress that flared around her knees. It made her look feminine and soft, and with her hair down and wavy...

He didn't know what to do with the attraction that welled almost violently inside him, riding the tide of his rioting adrenaline and blood pressure.

He backed up a step and used one hand to take off his hat; the other he swept through his hair, hoping the motion might hide any hint of the turmoil he was experiencing.

"What were you doing outside?" he barked.

"I was coming to look for you. Matt said he thought you were still in the barn. It's suppertime."

Suppertime. When was the last time someone had cared enough to make sure he came in for supper? Something twisted in his stomach.

But the fear he'd felt when he'd seen her out in the open remained.

His nostrils flared as he contemplated what he might do to his brother. "He should've told you to stay inside. Why didn't you just call my cell?"

Carrie was still approaching, waving a wooden spoon in his direction. "I was watching through the window and saw you barrel into Allie. Her head hit the wall pretty hard—I heard the *clunk* from inside."

Had he done that?

"Can you give us a minute?" he asked his sister, and if the words weren't completely polite, Carrie must've seen in his expression that he was shaken up, because she disappeared into the kitchen.

He moved in close to Alessandra again, tossing his hat on a nearby hook before he reached for her. One hand cupped her shoulder while he threaded his other hand through the hair at her nape, feeling for a bump.

Crap. The sweater was as soft as it looked. And her hair was even softer.

"I'm sorry if I hurt you." He said the words more to distract himself than anything else.

It didn't work.

"I'll be all right." From this close, her softly-spoken words were only a puff of air against his chin. "I thought I was safe here."

He didn't feel a bump or abrasion on the back of her head, but for some reason his hand got stuck there, cupping the back of her head like a boyfriend might hold a girlfriend.

He read the questions and lingering fear in her expressive eyes. "I got a call from one of my buddies and there's still some noise that your family remains a target. I don't have any evidence that someone is *here*, but..."

Her lip trembled, slightly. And for a prolonged moment, he really wanted to lean in and kiss her. Wanted it so bad that he let go of her completely and stepped back, so quickly that she wobbled and had to steady herself with one hand against the wall.

What was he even thinking? He was sweaty and smelled like horses from working out in the barn. He was probably the last person on earth that she'd be interested in kissing.

"I don't know..." He turned his back and ran a hand through his hair again. What was it about her that shook him up so badly? "It could be nothing, but I've got a feeling. Like something's coming."

He dared to look at her, hoping he wouldn't see an expression that meant she thought he was crazy.

She didn't. She looked slightly steadier than she had earlier, her eyes more clear.

"We don't know each other very well, but I trust you," she said. "If you want me to take more precautions, I will. Although I haven't stepped foot outside since yesterday. Until..." She nodded to the door, and he remembered the feeling of her pressed against him on the other side of that wall. Remembered too well.

And the fear that had caused it.

He nodded. "I appreciate it." He couldn't let himself think about something happening to her.

Alessandra relied on every stitch of media training she'd ever had to present a calm facade as she preceded Gideon into the kitchen.

He'd been frightened when he'd barreled into her outside. She'd felt it in the intentionality of his compact movements.

It was hard to imagine what might frighten someone like Gideon, who was so very much a soldier, so sure of himself. That in itself was scary.

That fear remained with her now.

Whether the danger was real or not, he'd shielded her completely. She'd been under a protective detail hundreds of times, but she'd never had she felt so totally safe.

And then, in the mudroom... She'd thought for a moment that he would kiss her.

She'd wanted him to. Wanted to know what it felt like to be kissed by someone as virile and alive as Gideon.

Oh, she'd had a few first kisses. The rare second one. The men her father would approve of were groomed and polished. Boring. She dealt with political and social issues on a daily basis. Didn't want her dating life to revolve around them.

Until now, she hadn't known what she'd been missing.

If she'd been braver, she might've used the opportunity to stretch up on tiptoes and kiss *him*. But she'd chickened out.

All Gideon had seen from her was a scared rabbit, one who knew how to clean. So what? He hadn't seen how eloquent she could be. Hadn't seen her passion for children—her mostly-secret passion, as she didn't have enough time to devote to the charities she really wanted to help.

He'd probably rebuff her if she got up the courage

to kiss him.

He stopped short in the kitchen, hanging back where the bright lights changed from the mudroom and hallway to the kitchen proper.

Carrie was at the stove, stirring the pot of chili they'd worked on together earlier. Alessandra could hear Scarlett giving some of the hands a preschool lesson in the dining room.

But it was Dan and Trey that Gideon was staring at. As if he'd never seen them before. "What—?"

Both men were clean shaven, and Carrie had given them both haircuts before supper. They looked completely different—in fact, Alessandra had startled at first when she'd walked into the hall and spotted Trey earlier. They even wore button-up shirts over their jeans that seemed to be freshly laundered. In the dining room, she'd seen that Brian and Chase had done the same.

"I brought my shears out from the shop this afternoon. They clean up pretty good, don't they?" Carrie asked. She patted Trey—nearest her—on the shoulder.

Alessandra looked between the Trey and Gideon, who seemed to be having some kind of stare-off contest.

"Any reason you pokes decided to get all gussied up? Today?" There was a slightly menacing tone in

Gideon's words, one that would have had her cowering in her shoes if it had been aimed at her.

But Trey's chin jerked even higher. "Pretty ladies coming around makes a man want to look his best, boss."

"Maybe the *ladies* won't be hanging around for long," Gideon growled.

Carrie crossed her arms over her chest, aiming a glance that was almost belligerent toward her brother. "*I* think it's about time."

Gideon made an incoherent sound beneath his breath, and Alessandra had to pinch her lips together to keep from smiling. Carrie had told her earlier that her big brother was overprotective, but Alessandra hadn't gotten to see it in action until now. She couldn't help but wonder at the interplay among Gideon, his sister, and Trey.

Dan had wisely slipped into the dining room when he'd seen Gideon's thunderous expression.

"What about you, Gideon?" Carrie asked, her words almost a taunt. She used the first two fingers of one hand to make a clipping motion. "How long has it been since you've had a cut?"

Gideon shot an inscrutable look in Alessandra's direction before he shook his head tightly at his sister. "Not tonight."

"Gideon's probably hungry," Alessandra put in,

wanting to ease the strange tension that had built at Carrie's last comment. "He didn't come in for lunch."

She moved to dish him a deep bowl of chili, nudging Carrie out of the way. The other woman slipped her arm through Trey's, and they escaped into the front hall, bypassing the dining room. The cadence of their low conversation carried, but not the actual words.

"You don't have to cook for us," he said, shouldering in next to her and running water to scrub his hands in the sink.

The scent of sharp spices rose to her as she ladled out the meat and beans.

"And I don't have to clean for you," she returned, holding out the bowl and a spoon upright for him. "It makes me feel useful."

He finished drying his hands and tucked the towel back in its holder above the sink. One eyebrow quirked. "You have a hard time relaxing? Ever go on vacation?"

A slow blush burned her cheeks, but she met his gaze squarely. She was used to her life being scheduled. Tightly packed with activities. It wasn't anything to be ashamed of. "Sometimes it's easier to stay busy."

He couldn't know how true it was, especially when living with her father and older sister. The truth was, she'd felt more affection from the cowboys and Carrie here than she had in years with her own family. Being on the Triple H felt like *home*.

So cleaning up a little and cooking didn't feel like chores. It felt like giving back to the people who'd helped her, who'd made her feel welcome.

~ * ~

For the second night in a row, Alessandra couldn't sleep. Not only did she have to contend with the images of Tim's death, but now there was the worry of someone coming after her here, on Gideon's land. After the boisterous supper and some visiting with the cowboys before bedtime, once everything had quieted, she couldn't forget those moments with Gideon's on the back porch.

She'd run to save her life, but had she managed to put Gideon and his family's and employees' lives in danger?

She crept down to the first floor, once again to the cadence of snoring cowboys in the upstairs hallway.

But this time, when she hit the bottom step, an arm like an iron band wrapped around her waist, and a hand clamped over her mouth.

She panicked and a shriek rose in her throat. Would anyone even hear her with her mouth and nose blocked?

"Ssh."

The hand moved away from her mouth, while the arm remained.

She opened her mouth to scream when the man's scent and presence registered. *Gideon.*

Heart thrumming like a hummingbird's wings, she struggled to draw breath. Her knees weak from fright, the band of his arm was the only thing holding her upright.

He whispered a rough word. "I didn't mean to scare you. Matt's just outside the back door. I think he's on the phone. I was trying to hear his conversation."

She panted through the pounding of her heart but couldn't manage to catch her breath.

He seemed to realize exactly how shaken up she was, because he gently turned her toward him, though the embrace was loose, with space between their bodies. "Sorry," he murmured. "Sorry."

One of his hands came up to cup her cheek, his chapped skin warm against her chilled self.

"Alessandra..."

He breathed her name—her real name. It was the first time she'd heard it since she'd been on the ranch. And then, as if he couldn't help himself, he bent his head toward her and kissed her.

Earlier, she'd wondered what it would feel like to be kissed by Gideon. The reality was like being swept away in a tsunami. Blood rushed to her face at the first brush of his lips against hers. His mouth slanted gently but firmly against hers as his nose brushed her cheek. She'd expected his beard to feel stiff and bristly, but instead it was soft, his mustache tickling her upper lip. She smiled into the kiss, and he drew away slightly, leaving only a breath between their lips.

She brushed his upper lip with her index finger. Whispered, "I've never kissed a man with a beard before."

She was close enough to make out the slight flare of his nostrils before he lowered his head to hers once more. This time he deepened the kiss, and she was lost in a wave of swirling warmth.

Too soon, he drew away, pressing his cheek against hers.

"Sorry," this time he breathed the word against her cheek.

Sorry for scaring her, or for kissing her?

Her trembling had steadied, but now her body hummed with something else entirely. "I thought..." She tried to speak, but her voice emerged wobbly. "I thought someone had gotten inside."

He moved slightly away, holding her loosely now. He used one hand to brush a strand of hair out of her face. "No one's going to get inside. Apollo would sound an alert."

She heard the dog's snuffle of a snore from somewhere else in the house. Maybe from near the front door?

"He didn't bark when I came downstairs," she pointed out.

She sensed more than saw him smile in the dark. "I asked the hands to set up a watch. Someone'll be awake at all times during the night. Nobody's getting inside. Matt's on first."

She exhaled a breath that was slightly less shaky. "Why were you spying on your brother?"

She felt tension through the links of his arms still around her. She still couldn't see his face. There was a long pause before he answered. "I think something is wrong. Maybe it's a woman or maybe something happened just before he got sent home on leave."

"Have you asked him about it?" It was a terribly impertinent question, but it slipped out anyway.

"Tried," came the short answer. "He's not being real forthcoming."

"How sure are you?"

If anything, the tension in him increased. "It's nothing I can put my finger on. Just a..."

"Feeling." She waited for him to say something more, but he remained silent. So she offered, "Maybe he'll open up when he's ready."

She couldn't see Gideon's face, but could almost imagine the skeptical twist of his lips, though he didn't make a sound.

"He's an adult," she whispered, feeling as if she were stepping over the line with the statement. But it was true. It was admirable that Gideon cared what was going on with his brother, but Matt didn't have to tell his brother anything. It—whatever it was— was his burden to bear.

Gideon didn't respond, and she was afraid she *had* overstepped.

Then he shook her slightly. "There's nothing left for you to clean. You should be sleeping."

"I haven't tackled the living room windows yet," she teased softly. Then, in a whisper. "I...can't sleep. Every time I start to drift off, I see..." *Tim.*

His hands tightened infinitesimally where they rested on her waist.

She swallowed hard. "My...my mom died when I was young, but I don't really remember..."

A breath passed between them.

"This was different," he said, and his voice was rough. "It was violent. Traumatic."

She nodded, throat closing up.

"It will take some time. The memories will start to lose their power. You won't forget, but the sharpness of those moments will fade. You'll be able to divert your thoughts. Sleep better."

"Really?" She could barely fathom it.

"Yeah." He must've sensed that she needed extra reassurance because he went on. "One of the first missions I went on... We were sent in covertly to rescue this hostage. Our cover was blown."

She could tell from the deepening timber of his voice that it was hard for him to talk about this. She rested her palms gently against his muscled chest, wanting to offer comfort. She was more than a little impressed by the strength she felt beneath her hands.

"We got out, but the hostage was shot. He bled out in my hands. I didn't sleep for a week. Spent some time talking to the shrink assigned to the Teams. Still had trouble turning it off, but after awhile...it got easier."

His story ended, and she could hear the rough breaths as he exhaled. She couldn't see his face—no doubt he was thankful for that—but she still knew that re-telling these events had reopened the wound he felt. Because there was more to the man this his gruff, powerful demeanor.

"Thank you for telling me," she said. It seemed so inadequate for what he'd given her.

Knowing that a strong, powerful man like Gideon was, in fact, as human as she was a comfort. It likely wouldn't help her to sleep tonight, or tomorrow night, but she was glad he'd shared with her.

"Is that why you're worried about Matt? Are you afraid something like that happened to him?"

He exhaled, the puff of warm air brushing her forehead. "I guess. After what happened during my last tour—my stepdad died—now it's up to me to take care of the family."

It was a nice thought, but... Matt and Carrie were adults, each with their own lives. The ranch was well-run, with a foreman and plenty of hands. Was Gideon's sense of caretaking verging on overprotective?

She didn't know the whole situation. Had only known Gideon for two days. How could she make a judgment? She couldn't.

Suddenly the back door opened, and there was the sound of motion as Matt must have stepped inside. "Gid?"

Gideon cleared his throat. "Yeah."

The kitchen light flipped on, and Gideon stepped away from Alessandra, his arms finally falling away.

"Uh... am I interrupting something?" Matt's voice wasn't loud, but it carried a definite note of amusement.

"No," Gideon said firmly. Although if Matt had come in minutes earlier, he definitely would've been interrupting. "Allie can't sleep, and I thought I'd take her with me out to the barn."

Matt stared at his brother, an enigmatic expression crossing his face.

"Not for too long," Gideon insisted.

Matt shrugged. "This is your mission, brother. Do what you want."

Glad she'd pulled on a pair of jeans and warm, woolen socks with the long-sleeved T-shirt she'd worn to bed, Alessandra followed Gideon to the mudroom as Matt changed places with them, arms crossed over his chest as he watched from the hallway.

"You can borrow one of mine, even though it'll swallow you up." Gideon pulled a heavy brown corduroy coat from a hook on the wall and held it open for her. She stuffed her arms in the sleeves. Her hands didn't even poke through the ends, and the coat hung past her thighs.

He tugged, turning her back toward him, before he looped a scratchy knitted scarf over her neck and began tucking the front ends in a loose knot.

"Um..." She lifted her right foot to show the woolen socks.

His mouth quirked. "We've got an old pair of Carrie's boots here." He bent, rifling among the boots lined up against the wall, finally coming up with a pair of what looked like a cross between rain boots and work boots. "They might be a little big."

She had to hold onto his shoulder as he helped her step into the boots. And if she held on a moment too long, well...who could blame her?

LACY WILLIAMS

CHAPTER SEVEN

Gideon knew this was a bad idea. Spending time alone with Alessandra. Getting close to her.

Definitely kissing her had been a bad idea.

But he couldn't seem to help himself, not when she'd been shaken by the memories of what had happened to her in New York. He knew what that was like.

And...okay. His motives weren't entirely altruistic.

The more time he spent with her, the more he liked her. She was a good listener. Didn't tell him he was foolish to be spying on his brother.

Getting involved with someone who was leaving felt like the most dangerous thing he'd done since he'd left the Teams.

But he couldn't seem to help himself.

He hustled her across the expanse of yard between the house and barn. *If* someone was watching the place, they probably wouldn't be expecting to see the princess coming outside at this time of night. And he'd bundled her up pretty good.

It only took seconds to jog across the space with Alessandra tucked under his arm, and then they reached the barn.

"You'll want to keep your coat on," he cautioned as he pulled the door closed. Although the building offered the protection from the cutting wind, only the office was heated, and not by much.

She followed him in, looking all around, her face open with curiosity and wonder. Her nose wrinkled adorably.

"You don't like the smell?" he teased.

"Now I understand why all the cowboys have been heading for the shower first thing before supper," she retorted. She smiled. *Smiled!* "It's the scent of your trade," she said with a little shrug. "It isn't disgusting."

He didn't know about that. "Glad you think so, but I'd still advise watching your step."

"What do you do out here at night?" she asked. "Aren't the animals sleeping?"

He led the way to the plank fence that separated them from the open part of the barn, where a mama and her new baby did, in fact, sleep. Opposite, a second cow circled in an agitated manner. Her belly was distended and judging by her movements, she was close.

"It's calving season." He motioned her to join him at the railing. "Right now we've got several new babies being born every day." He leveled a look at her. "And some at night. We track the cows that are close and try to get them into the barn, so we can watch them and make sure there aren't any complications with the birth."

"Are there often complications?"

He shrugged. "Sometimes. We help out if we can, get the vet out here if it turns into an emergency situation." He nodded to the cow who had now lain in the hay. "This little lady looks like she's close. If I'm right, you can watch a little miracle."

She leaned both elbows on the railing. Her hands weren't visible in the coat at all, it swallowed her up. But he'd felt a visceral *Mine!* when he'd tucked her into the coat a few minutes earlier.

"It seems like a lot of sleepless night," she said with a sideways glance at him.

"For about a month. Maybe six weeks." He shrugged. "It's part of running a cattle operation."

"It must be vastly different than what you used to do—in the military."

He nodded. "It is. More cyclical. A lot less training required."

But she didn't seem to appreciate his humor. "Do you ever miss it? Being on assignment? Going into danger?"

Being on high alert this week had certainly reminded him of what he'd left behind. He missed being an important part of the team, having a critical assignment that meant the life or death of the mission.

"Doesn't matter. My knee blew out on my last mission. I wouldn't be fit for active duty anymore." And that killed him. He kept his focus on the cow, aware of Alessandra's gaze on his face. The cow was straining, obviously in the throes of labor, but nothing seemed to be happening.

"Besides," he said offhandedly, "someone's got to run this place. And Carrie and the squirt need me."

She slanted a look at him. "It seems as if Trey might be angling for the *she-needs-me* position in Carrie's life."

He grunted. "He'd better not be."

"Why not? He works for you. You've got to have some trust in him." Her statement was innocent, but it didn't help the acid churning in his gut.

"After what happened to her, Carrie needs someone..." He searched for the right word, but it wasn't coming to him easily.

"Who makes a better living than a cowhand?" she asked, turning to face him. "Who's more trustworthy? Good-looking? From a better background?"

He matched her stance, looking right down on her. "None of those."

Her head tilted to the side. "Then what?"

He ran a hand over his beard. "Two years ago, while I was on my last mission, my uncle died. Carrie's ex-husband had been gone since before Scarlett was born. But all of a sudden, he showed up. Thought she stood to get a big inheritance and tried to pound it out of her. By the time he was done, she had a concussion, broken arm, and two busted ribs."

It still made him sick to think about it. He'd been gone, and Carrie had been helpless.

Alessandra touched him, cupped his elbow in one hand. Brought him back from that dark place when he'd been laid up in the hospital, barely able to move for his knee, knowing nobody was there to take care of his sister.

"I think it's admirable that you want to be there for Carrie, but..." She bit her lip, looking down. "She is a grown woman. She can date—or marry—whomever she wants."

He knew that. He just wanted her to pick a winner this time. And while he'd known Trey for years, he wasn't sure the hand was the right guy for his sister.

He looked back to the cow, saw she was still in distress. "I've got to go in there and check her out."

~ * ~

Alessandra watched Gideon hop the fence and move to the cow lying prostrate in the hay.

"So now you've got the dish about Carrie. I want to know why your aunt is targeting your family."

She shivered, burrowing deeper into the coat. "I've never met my aunt, and my father doesn't like to talk about her."

"They don't get along?" He'd approached the cow's *derrière* and squatted there. From where she stood, she couldn't see exactly what he was doing.

"My father has...some challenges. It isn't publicized, but he's battled MS for years. It's terminal, and he's getting worse every day."

A few moments passed as he looked over the cow.

"That must be hard," he finally said.

It was. More so because she wanted things to be different. She'd hoped that being faced with his mortality would mean that her father would spend more time with her and her sisters. That she could get to know the *man* and not the *king*.

But instead, he'd pushed each of the three girls to work harder for the kingdom in the name of family duty. He'd insisted on carrying out his duties as much as possible. Because most of the burden of her father's illness fell on Eloise, Alessandra often felt invisible to her father.

There was a rush of fluid and blood and a little black body plopped into the hay near Gideon's feet. Gideon reached for clumps of hay and began rubbing, drying the little body.

The calf floundered in the hay for moments, and then mama and baby both managed their feet, and Gideon backed slowly away.

He returned to where she stood, hopping the fence again and standing elbow-to-elbow with her at the railing.

Although he watched as the mama licked her baby all over, she knew Gideon's attention was still focused on her.

"What about your security team?" Gideon asked. "Have there been any heightened threats lately? Phone calls to the palace? Letters?"

She was ashamed that she didn't know. "Not that I've been briefed on."

"No ex-boyfriends with an agenda?"

She turned her head to meet his sideways glance straight on. "No ex-boyfriends." She'd had dates, sometimes multiple dates, but no one serious enough to call a boyfriend.

Had he asked out of concern about the shooting, or was he fishing?

She raised her brows at him. "What about you?

Did your last girlfriend break your heart? There's no one special for you?"

He frowned, eyes on the cow and calf. "I didn't date while on the Teams. It's hard on girlfriends not to know where your man is or if he'll come back. Hang on."

He went back into the pen, approaching the mama and baby slowly.

The cow bellowed at him, and he froze a few feet in.

"What's wrong?" she whispered.

"The calf should be suckling by now," he answered over his shoulder. "She's not helping it out. And she doesn't seem to want to let me get close."

He didn't elaborate. He attempted to get close to the animals twice more, but the cow lowered its head when he neared, and he backed off, returned to the fence near Alessandra.

She'd seen that thundercloud expression on his face before.

"What will happen, then?" Alessandra worried aloud. "Will the calf—?"

"If she rejects it, we'll likely end up bottle-feeding the thing. Which is a huge pain."

His focus was still on the animals, and he didn't see the twitch of her lips.

He might be gruff, but she was learning to see

beyond it. He was soft enough to care if the calf lived or died, and not just for the money. He might complain about having to feed the calf, but she knew he would do it.

He was just that kind of cowboy.

LACY WILLIAMS

CHAPTER EIGHT

Over the next few days, Gideon watched as Alessandra seem to thrive in ranch life.

With no further sign of anyone on their property, no noise from local law enforcement, and Cash assuring him that the reports they were getting didn't have Alessandra's whereabouts located anywhere near north Texas, he no longer kept her confined to the house.

She spent hours in the barn, bottle-feeding the calf she'd dubbed Valentine.

She cooked and cleaned up after the hands, no matter how much he chided her to do otherwise. Where, before her arrival, the hands had been rowdy and willing to let their appearance and behavior slide, they were more polite and cleaned up each night before supper. She'd changed them for the better.

Once, he caught her watching a national news broadcast with a pensive look on her face, but other than that, she seemed content.

He, however, was a boiling mess of emotions.

He couldn't seem to keep himself from sneaking kisses. In the barn. After supper, while she corralled him to dry dishes for her. He found her addictive, especially when she smiled a secret little smile after he'd kissed her—a smile he hadn't seen her give to anyone else.

He'd even trimmed his beard. He hadn't shaved it, because she seemed to like it.

But all the while, he reminded himself that she wasn't here to stay, no matter how well she seemed to fit into his life.

She was used to the jet-set lifestyle. Fancy parties. Events where she rubbed elbows with famous people.

She would eventually marry a prince.

Not an ex-Navy SEAL with a ruined knee and obligations that tied him to the family ranch.

Somehow, he'd become uncomfortable in his own life as well. He needed to keep Alessandra safe. He'd accepted it as his own personal mission. So he left Nate with more responsibility, so he could scout their land and the neighbors close by.

Though he'd relaxed a little, allowing Alessandra to the barn, he didn't trust that things had gone quiet. Every so often, he got that awful feeling down the back of his neck and shoulders, like someone was watching.

Waiting.

Biding their time.

Like he'd do, if he was tasked with taking out the princess.

It just made him more itchy, being out of the loop. Relying on the Glorvaird and New York enforcement agencies. Not being in on it.

And he wasn't a patient man.

Even through his distraction, the Triple H hadn't fallen down around their shoulders.

Was Matt right that Gideon had stunted Nate's potential by taking on too much responsibility for the ranch duties?

Worse, was Alessandra right that he'd done the same to Carrie? Had he kept his little sister from finding happiness because he'd been determined to fix every single thing that went wrong in her life?

He didn't know how to manage all of that.

He didn't know how to keep from getting hurt when Alessandra left. Where his place was, if it wasn't as the boss of the Triple H. Who needed him, if Carrie didn't? If he couldn't help Matt? If Nate could run the ranch without him?

He was anchorless. A SEAL without a team.

And then his phone rang.

~ * ~

Alessandra felt Gideon's heightened tension at supper. Almost as if he was pulling away from her.

After the meal, he drew her into the living room, leaving Matt and the hands behind at the dining table.

His expression was deadly serious as he said, "Your head of security called. They're ready for you to come home to Glorvaird."

She'd known it was coming, but the words were still unexpected. She wasn't ready yet. Valentine was only a few days old. And she was supposed to have lunch with Carrie on Friday.

And Gideon...

He was already heading for the door. "You'll want to pack up tonight. We'll leave early in the morning for the airport. They're sending you a new passport, which we'll pick up on the way."

And then he was gone, banging through the mudroom and out the back door.

She sat for a moment, heart pounding. Should she follow him?

She'd give him until the dishes were done to clear his mind.

But he didn't come back, not after the last dish had been washed and put away.

She waited in the living room, curled beneath an afghan as the house darkened around her. She let her eyes roam, noting the changes. She and Carrie had made them together. Photos of the Hales: Gideon, Matt, Carrie, and Scarlett, now lined the walls. A pitcher with hothouse flowers from town claimed space on the end table.

It wasn't the empty dreary room it had been when she'd arrived.

She'd like to think she'd brought changes to the people, too.

She idly played with the phone Gideon had given her, scanning through the pictures on the high-tech device. She'd surreptitiously taken several candid photos of Gideon when he hadn't been watching. Him working with the cattle, actively shooing two mama cows and their days-old babies back out into the open pasture. Laughing from across the supper table at something Matt had said. She rarely saw those genuine smiles cross Gideon's face, much less his entire face lit and open with laughter. Mostly when he interacted with his family, though a few times his expression had been open and soft after they'd kissed.

She traced the line of his smile with the tip of her finger. She was falling in love with the irascible cowboy.

She'd thought something real was growing between them. Which was why his absence tonight confused and hurt her.

At ten, she decided not to wait any longer. She was a princess, wasn't she? Capable of standing up for herself. Facing hard things, not cowering. She'd find Gideon and tell him how she felt. They couldn't leave things like this. Unresolved.

All the cowhands were upstairs in bed, except for Nate, who nursed a cup of coffee as he stood in front of the kitchen window, looking out.

She'd already bundled up in the heaviest sweater Carrie had loaned her and thick wool socks. "I'm going to run out to the barn," she told the hand, whose eyes twinkled with merriment.

"I'll keep an eye out," he promised.

She slipped into Carrie's old work boots and Gideon's coat, bundling up as best she could before she darted across the yard.

Something felt different tonight.

She was aware of Nate standing on the back porch, watching her cross to the barn. But somehow, without Gideon beside her, the darkness felt menacing. The cold felt threatening.

Was her mind making things up because of the anticipation of leaving tomorrow? She'd found safety, an inkling of peace on the ranch.

Wind rushed at her back, and she misjudged the final few feet, running into the door with a *thump*. She straightened, not hurt but a little shaken at the way she'd let her imagination take off. When she tugged on the door, it wouldn't budge.

And then it did, almost ripping from her hands. Gideon stood there, inches from her.

His face was dark as he pulled her inside the lit space, throwing a glare over her shoulder.

"What the—?" He mumbled what she thought was an expletive before releasing her. She reeled a few feet away. "You walked out here in the dark, alone?"

"I ran," she said. "And Nate was watching from the porch. Besides... aren't you taking the bodyguard thing a little far? I thought things were safe now."

He muttered something else beneath his breath. "Just because nothing's happened doesn't mean you're safe. It could mean the threat has gone underground."

It was a valid point. She'd had no sense that anything had been wrong in New York City, either. Gideon was the soldier.

"I'm sorry."

Her apology didn't seem to ease his tension. His Stetson was pulled low over his eyes, and he backed a few feet farther from her.

She wrapped her arms around her middle under the pretense of holding the coat together. "If you'd come inside earlier, I wouldn't have had to come looking for you."

"Shouldn't you be in bed by now?" he muttered.

"Shouldn't you?" she returned. Then, softer, "I need to talk to you."

"Why?" he asked, voice flat. "Why are we still pretending when you're going home tomorrow?"

His words stung. "Pretending?" It had all been real to her. Every moment with Gideon had brought a sense of belonging.

Until now.

"I can't do it anymore." The hardness in his voice was like being struck, and she clutched herself tighter. "Pretend that all of this is going to have a happy ending."

A muscle ticked away in his jaw, proving he wasn't as emotionless as he let on.

She took a deep breath, searching for the right words.

"I've been doing some thinking," she said, heart thrumming loudly in her ears. "We might come from different places, but that doesn't mean we can't be together—"

He laughed, a harsh sound. "Are you going to ditch your family and stay on the ranch? I know you've been enjoying yourself, but what about Dear Old Dad? What about your *obligations*?" His words were a verbal punch. She'd confided in him that she often felt stifled by her royal duties. That she wished for a closer relationship with her father. And now he was throwing her words back at her.

She shivered at the twist of his lips. Why was he being this way?

"You know I wouldn't be able to stay on all time. But if we split our time—"

"Split our time?"

She jerked her chin up. "You are more than the Triple H. You're well spoken and intelligent. Well-traveled. You could hold your own with any of the dignitaries I've met."

He looked dumbfounded. "You want me to go with you?"

"Like I said, we could split our time—"

But he was already shaking his head. "I can't leave. I've got to be here to look after the ranch—"

"That's Nate's job," she reminded him softly. She could see from the set of his shoulders that she wasn't getting through.

"What if something happened to Carrie again, and I was half the globe away?"

And she could see the guilt eating him up, still.

"What if you were half the globe away, and *nothing*

happened?" she asked gently. "What if you're giving up your chance at a different life for a hypothetical?"

He took off his hat and ran his hand through his hair, a gesture she knew meant he was upset.

"My whole life has been planned out for me, up until now," she said, wishing, praying that he could understand. "I never had a reason to fight for anything different, until now. Until you."

Hat still clutched in one hand, he looked at her. She could see the torment in his eyes. "I just don't see how it would work, long-term."

"But..." *She loved him.* The words stuck in her throat at the resigned look on his face.

"It makes sense that the ranch has been a place of rest for you. Something totally different than what you're used to. And a place that's kept you safe. But in six months, or next year during calving season... the newness will wear off. Even if you split your time..."

She noticed he didn't use the word *we*.

"You'll figure out this place is all work, work, and more *work*. *We*"—he pointed back and forth between them—"won't work. Not for long."

She didn't know how he'd become so defeated. Did he really think they were that different, after all she'd tried to do to prove to him that she could be a cowgirl, too?

Tears rose, and she valiantly fought them back. Her heart might be breaking, but she didn't want him to see, not now that he'd rejected her.

"I'll see you home," he said, and she couldn't look at him. "But that's it. That's all it can be."

~ * ~

Gideon wasn't his best self the next morning, not after tossing and turning for hours.

He couldn't erase the image of Alessandra holding herself together last night, her hands shaking as she clutched her elbows.

As if, by denying that they could have something lasting together, he'd broken her.

The SEALs had taught him the value of considering every angle, every scenario, every possible ending. He couldn't see a way forward that didn't end with one of them in heartbreak—most likely him.

He feared his heart might be breaking now. He felt nauseated, like something he'd eaten last night hadn't set well with him.

She'd been quiet on the ride to Dallas, once again sandwiched between him and Matt in the truck. He'd spent the entire drive watching for a tail, unconvinced she was safe, and fighting the icy roads.

There was no tail, but he still had that awful feeling down the back of his neck.

The airport was bustling as he pulled into the underground parking lot where this had all started. She slid out of the truck after him, and when as he helped her to the ground, he got his first good look at her of the morning. She wore a long, elegant coat similar to the one she'd worn that very first day. It fell open, revealing a slim pantsuit and heels— though not as unwieldy as the stone-encrusted ones they'd found her in. She looked night-and-day different from the farm girl who'd worn her hair in a braid and donned one of his flannel shirts when she fed the undernourished calf. Carrie must've gone shopping on her behalf, though they still hadn't let his sister in on "Allie's" secret identity.

He and Matt flanked her as they walked inside.

"Keep your eyes open," he told his brother, though it wasn't necessary. At least Matt seemed to be taking this seriously, scanning the crowds as they passed through the lower-level corridor and then arrived at the passenger check-in. Because Gideon had printed her boarding pass at home, they were able to move directly to the Security line. He'd coordinated with the royal security team and planned to accompany her to New York, then hop a flight right back home. Matt would kill time around here, and they'd drive back to the Triple H together.

This was the end of his time with Alessandra.

She hugged Matt at the Security line, then walked through, that princess-grace evident in her posture, her calm exterior.

Gideon stayed close, silent, like a bodyguard would. Which felt appropriate, since she still wasn't speaking to him.

She clutched his cell phone between her hands, though he didn't know why.

Inside the terminal, they discovered the flight had been delayed as the airport personnel de-iced the runway. He growled quietly. It was only an hour's delay, but it meant more time out in the open.

The hair on the back of his neck was tingling again, this time the pit of his stomach carried a knot the size of a boulder.

The gate attendant confirmed the delay, and he stifled the urge to punch someone.

"Can we get something to eat?" the princess asked.

He agreed reluctantly.

Everyone else seemed to have the same idea, because the few food places that were open on their end of the terminal were packed. Alessandra stood in line for a bakery kiosk, him beside her.

The feeling on the back of his neck got worse. He

kept Alessandra close to his side, noticing and hating it when she unobtrusively put a few inches between them.

He craned his neck, trying to see in all directions. Could someone have snuck a gun inside the airport, where security was tight? Or a knife? He knew it could happen, but...

There. Near the restrooms, a man in a long trench coat was darting looks in all directions, one hand tucked beneath his coat. Gideon lost focus on the crowd around them as he zeroed in on the suspicious guy.

"Sorry the lines are so long," an older, feminine voice said from nearby. "Would you like to try one of our apple fritters? It's a free sample."

Gideon turned back to the princess, just in time to see her take a paper-wrapped pastry from a uniformed woman. He didn't get a good look at the woman's face, only the dingy gray ponytail hanging from the back of her ballcap.

Focus now split between Trench-coat Guy and the woman who'd approached Alessandra, Gideon lost a half-second of reaction time.

"Wait—"

But he was too late to stop the princess from raising the tissue-wrapped pastry to her mouth. She ate a bite.

Still distracted by Trench-coat Guy, he put his hand beneath Alessandra's elbow. "Can we sit down now?" He didn't wait for an answer.

They didn't make it back.

"Gideon, I'm—"

Alessandra faltered mid-step, and the only reason he was able to catch her around the waist was because he'd been so close to her.

What was happening?

Her eyelids fluttered rapidly, and her cheeks were reddening as he watched. She collapsed, and the pastry she'd held dropped to the floor.

Panic threading through his veins, he knelt, cradling her head. "Alessandra. Honey?"

He searched for a pulse even as she lost consciousness.

"Help!" he called out, waving down the gate attendant. "I need medical help!"

He touched her beneath the coat, feeling for any sign of a bullet entry, though there was no blood blooming, and he'd heard no *pop*, even from a gunshot that had been silenced.

Had she been poisoned? The thought was absurd, but what else could've happened?

Fear clawed through him at her weak, fluttering pulse.

He was supposed to have protected her.

How could he have let this happen?

CHAPTER NINE

Hours later, Gideon sat beside Alessandra's hospital bed in the secure ICU wing of the university hospital, head in his hands.

He'd been praying, frantic wordless prayers, since the princess had been poisoned at the airport. He'd believed the royal security team when they'd said the danger was past. Hadn't given enough credence to his gut.

Someone had gotten close enough to *poison* her.

And Gideon had let it happen.

The doctors had praised his quick thinking as he'd scooped up the remainder of the apple pastry into a plastic baggie before they'd rushed Alessandra out of the airport on a medevac helicopter. First, they'd pumped her stomach. Initial testing of the pastry had identified large doses of cyanide, and the doctors had quickly given her an anti-cyanide antidote kit.

She'd remained unconscious since the airport. It was probably a blessing for her not to be awake to feel the poison ravaging her body, but Gideon wished and prayed for nothing more than her to open those bright blue eyes and look at him.

He pinched the bridge of his nose, hoping to stem the tears that burned behind his nose.

In all the chaos, with his adrenaline pumping, he'd felt the same clarity he had back when he was with the Teams on a mission. The high-octane situation had burned away all his excuses, all the worries that had once seemed so important that they'd clouded his judgment. And his true feelings.

He loved her.

And all the rest of it didn't matter.

She'd been right. They could figure things out with their schedules, the ranch, his siblings.

None of that mattered when all he could see was her closed eyes, her motionless body.

He just wanted to *be* with her. For any time they could carve out to spend together, for now, forever.

But first, she had to wake up. The doctors and nurses were monitoring her closely, but they wouldn't be able to fully evaluate how much damage the cyanide had done until she regained consciousness.

A knock at the door brought his head up, though it felt as if it weighed a thousand pounds.

While the ER doctors had been working to save her life, he'd coordinated with local law enforcement and the nearest high-clearance security team he could find to set up this secure wing in the hospital. Where before he'd been content to let the royal security team manage things from offsite, he refused to risk her life again, not when he could do something about it.

Carrie stuck her head around the door, and he stood, surprise overcoming the lethargy in his limbs. "What're you doing here?"

"Matt called." She stepped inside as he reached for her, and her arms came around him in a hug that had him blinking against his burning eyes. "The guys are here, too, out in the waiting room."

He hugged her tightly, unable to find words. Alessandra had been right. He hadn't been able to protect her from right beside her. He needed to learn to let go and trust God and Carrie. She could handle her own life.

Even if it wasn't entirely comfortable right now.

"How is she?" Carrie asked.

"Unconscious." He ran a hand through his hair, missing his hat. It'd been lost somewhere in the melee. "It takes hours to run the full test on the poison she ingested, but the doctors think they've at least stopped it from doing further damage."

Carrie sniffled a little as she looked at Alessandra's pale face against the pillow, hair mussed and IVs trailing from Alessandra's arm.

Gideon's chest felt so full and hot that he wanted to howl.

Suddenly, more bodies were crowding inside. The ranch hands were led by Trey, who had his chin hitched in the air and a stubborn glint in his eyes. "Figured if y'all are holding a prayer vigil, we'd better all get in on it." He moved next to Carrie, one hand resting at her waist.

Gideon nodded once, letting the cowboy—and his friend—know that he couldn't protest a friendship or relationship anymore.

Matt came near, clapping him on the shoulder.

"The nurse know you're all in here? Probably against protocol." But for the moment, Gideon's will was too weak to protest more.

And then, Carrie and all the ranch hands had slung their arms around each other, circling the bed in one big man-hug as they bowed heads. On the end of the chain, Gideon gently laid his free hand on Alessandra's shoulder.

Each man shared a special prayer on Alessandra's behalf, beseeching God to heal her and bring her back to them.

By the time Dan had finished, every one of them was clearing his throat or surreptitiously wiping his eyes. They moved slightly away from each other and the brotherly intimacy of the moment, some of them shuffling their feet. Dan and Nate shoved their hats back on their heads.

"Is she really a princess?" Chase hooked his thumb over his shoulder.

Gideon glared at Matt, who raised his hands helplessly. "Sorry, man. Some reporter got shots while she was getting loaded into the helicopter."

Gideon winced.

"Got *pictures*," Matt corrected himself. "And by the time we got to the hospital, it was all over social media and local news stations."

That was a nightmare for another time. At least he'd had the foresight to secure this wing of the hospital.

"So she really is?" Chase pressed.

Gideon nodded. "Yeah."

Brian whistled low. "And we had her cleaning up after us like a maid."

Carrie's eyes were shining. "Scarlett will be thrilled. She's claimed this whole time that Allie was a princess."

Gideon rubbed the back of his neck with one hand. "She's not coming back to the Triple H. When she wakes up"—he almost choked on the words, but he had to believe she was going to wake up—"she's going back to Glorvaird."

Carrie looked at him with a glint of mischief in her eyes. "Maybe. I guess we'll see."

He clung to his sister's hope. Right now, it was all he had.

~ * ~

Alessandra was trapped in cold, terrifying darkness, unable to move. Barely able to think.

Voices came. Someone stuck something nasty down her throat and she gagged. The contents of her stomach emptied.

Oh, she *hated* being sick.

She was so hot.

No, *cold*.

And then came the voice of the man she loved. Gideon.

She even thought she heard Carrie, Matt, and the other hands. Were they...praying for her?

Peace and warmth stole over her. Snatches of conversation wafted to her, as if from far away.

"...she really a princess?"

"...she's going back to Glorvaird."

"Maybe..."

She couldn't go back. Not yet. There was still something undone. Something she hadn't told Gideon.

Why couldn't she wake up?

She needed...

She went cold again. Started shaking uncontrollably. Couldn't find her tongue.

And then there were voices again—strange ones. "She's seizing!"

Where had Gideon gone? Her friends?

She needed them.

Needed him.

Was lost.

~ * ~

It was after midnight, but Gideon couldn't sleep. The ICU room allowed for one uncomfortable chair, and the cowboys and his siblings had agreed to stay in the waiting room for now.

Why hadn't Alessandra woken?

Earlier, after the impromptu prayer vigil, she'd shown signs of improving.

And then she'd had some kind of seizure, her body reacting to the poison. The doctors had been able to help her ride it out, but since then, there'd been no sign of awareness behind her eyes. He imagined her lost in a deep pool. Maybe the seizure had brought her close to the surface. Since then, though, she seemed to have sunk all the way at the bottom, her beautiful heart hidden beneath the murky waves. Would she ever make it to the surface again?

Was he losing her? Was she drifting away even now as he watched her pale face?

This waiting...he was dying a slow death.

If she died, he would never be the same. He couldn't bear to think of a world where he wouldn't hear her laugh, see the flash of her teeth in that secret smile she'd only given to him.

He took her hand. Shook it gently. "Wake up, Allie-girl."

Nothing. No blip on the machines monitoring her. No catch of her breath.

"I need you—" His voice broke on the words. She'd never know how devastated he was at this moment, how very badly he'd realized he needed her.

"I was wrong. You were right." If ever there were words to wake a woman up...

And it was true. He'd been wrong to push her away. He should've been pulling her closer. They were a team, the two of them.

He waited. Still no change.

The clock ticked. The monitors proved she was still here, still with him. But still not.

"Please." He bowed his head over her hand, squeezed his eyes against the tears that were so close.

"Please." He didn't know what he was pleading for. For God not to take her, maybe. For her to come back to him.

Right now, thank you very much.

He rose from the chair, unable to contain the nervous energy that buzzed through him. He rested his hands against the railing and leaned over her, so pale and still in the bed. At least the awful red had faded from her skin, one of the signs of the cyanide poisoning.

"Alessandra," he breathed.

He leaned closer. Didn't even know what he was doing, but he had to do something.

He brushed one soft kiss, a feather kiss, again her mouth. One against her forehead. He let his chin rest against her temple.

And whispered, "I love you."

Alessandra felt Gideon's presence nearby, felt the brush of his whiskers against her temple.

"I love you."

She opened her eyes.

He froze. He backed slightly away, enough so she could see his dear face.

His hands were clamped around the hospital bed

railing, close enough that she barely had to move to reach for him. He met her grasp, his fingers tangling with hers.

"Alessandra." His breath caught, and there was no missing the sheen of tears in his eyes. Her sensitive *Bear.*

"Hi," she whispered, the word burning her throat. Tears stung her eyes.

He breathed out a shaky exhale, squeezed her hand once. He let go only to move away momentarily, and then he was back with a cup of water and a straw. He held it to her lips, and she drank greedily, feeling echoes of fever—or something—that had overwhelmed while she'd been lost in the darkness.

When she'd had her fill, he put away the cup. "I should call the nurse. There are a lot of people waiting for you to wake up."

He took her hand again and stared at her.

Long enough that she began to wonder what had happened. Had her hair been all shaved off? "What is it?"

He narrowed his eyes slightly. "For a bit there, I thought I might never see you looking back at me again."

"Was I sick?" she asked. "I remember feeling feverish, and cold. Choking. Throwing up."

"You were poisoned," he said. "You collapsed at the airport. The woman gave you that pastry... Remember?"

She did, barely.

"Mostly I remember you were going to let me walk away."

His eyes darkened, and he leaned close to touch his temple against hers. "That's because I was doing what my sex often does. Being an idiot."

Relief and love flowed through her. "So you've changed your mind, then? About us not *working* in the long-term?"

"Well, for one thing, your royal security team needs a massive overhaul. I can't trust them to get you back to Glorvaird safely, so it seems I'll be forced to accompany you at least that far."

He brushed a kiss against her upper cheek. "There's no telling how long it will take before they can be whipped into shape, and I can't leave you unprotected. You're too important." Though most of his words held a teasing note, those last were spoken with an intense seriousness.

"And then there's the fact that I've fallen in love with you," he said softly. "And I can't live without you. So I suppose the roundabout answer is: yes, I've changed my mind."

She raised her other hand, the first real movement

she'd made since waking. Everything seemed to be in working order, though she felt as weak as a baby. She cupped his cheek, his trimmed beard rough against her palm. "I'm in love with you, too."

His eyes squeezed shut, but not before she saw the depths of emotion that overwhelmed him.

"*That* seems like the second miracle of the day," he whispered. He brushed another gentle kiss against her lips. He drew away slightly, and her hand fell to the bed. "But if God wants to heap blessings on my head..."

She smiled. "You won't argue?"

"Not today."

He was forced to move back as a nurse and doctor bustled in, surprised to see her awake.

They began asking questions immediately, prodding her with a thermometer and stethoscope, but she held Gideon's gaze throughout.

It was a little bit astounding.

She'd never expected to be running for her life, then stranded on a working ranch for days on end. If not for New York, she never would have met Gideon.

Although he hadn't admitted to it, she guessed that if it hadn't been for Gideon's training and quick thinking, she could've died in the airport.

And then, he'd declared his love for her.

Miracles, indeed.

LACY WILLIAMS

EPILOGUE

"The Kissing Princess"

Mia, third in line to the Glorvaird crown, crumpled the newsprint between both hands.

She considered throwing it in the fire burning on the nearby hearth, but ultimately smoothed it out on the table. The headline shouted up at her again, making her lose any appetite for the breakfast spread laid out on a silver tray before her.

Is that what they really thought of her? All the public could see of her?

Beneath the headline was a photograph of her—yes, kissing—the young duke of Regis, a neighboring kingdom.

The long-range, slightly grainy photo didn't show the moments that followed, when she'd discovered his infidelity. The photograph didn't show the resounding slap she'd delivered.

The press liked to paint her as someone who hopped from boyfriend to boyfriend, who liked to play with men's hearts and give kisses freely, but it wasn't the truth. Not at all.

She fell in love easily. Too easily, as the line of jerks that had left her with a broken heart could attest to.

But the media didn't care about that.

Voices intruded, and she slouched in the wingback chair in the palace's blue parlor.

It sounded like her sister and her new—American—beau. She'd welcomed her sister back to the palace last night and met the handsome, dark-bearded man, but she didn't want company now. Maybe if she was quiet enough, still enough, they wouldn't find her here, and she could continue her sulk in private.

"You're having brunch with Eloise?" Gideon asked.

"Mm hmm. Worried about being left to your own devices?"

There was a quiet moment, and Mia squeezed her eyes closed, imagining her sister locking lips with the handsome American.

"Not too worried," came Gideon's voice, amused and warm. "I might sneak down and talk with your head of security while you're busy."

"Again?"

"There were a couple of recent email threats that

they should look into."

Mia's pulse sped momentarily. She'd been a part of the motorcade that the bombing had narrowly missed just three months ago. It had been the most frightening thing she'd ever experienced, and for brief seconds she'd thought she wouldn't survive. Since then, palace life had returned to a normal, if more vigilant, state.

She'd hoped that the threat was past, but it seemed Gideon didn't think so. Did he know something she didn't, or was his suspicion because of his former role as a soldier and the near-misses Alessandra had had?

"Stop *worrying* so much," Alessandra said to her beau. "You'll start to go prematurely gray, and then my people will think I'm dating a much older man."

"I'll stop *taking precautions* when I'm certain there are no threats against the woman I love."

It was a swoon-worthy statement. Mia's stomach twisted. Some of it was happiness for her sister. Some of it, she hated to admit, was envy. She wanted that kind of love for herself. Was desperate for it.

Her eyes fell to the front page again, as Alessandra and Gideon's voices faded to murmurs. Was it her imagination, or did her desperation show in the grainy photograph?

She couldn't go on like this. It wasn't healthy.

She needed to prove to herself—and to the kingdom—that she wasn't just the *kissing princess*.

And that's when she promised she would not kiss another man unless he was the man she would marry.

~ * ~

Gideon watched Alessandra disappear down the hall to meet her sister. He stood with both hands in the front pockets of his slacks, posture relaxed, just in case she turned around.

"I'll stop taking precautions when I'm certain there are no real threats against the woman I love."

He was fairly sure he'd convinced her that all he was thinking about was her security. Right now, nothing could be further from the truth.

When she turned the corner at the end of the opulent, marble-floored hall, he swiveled on his heel and marched back to the quarters he'd been assigned, in a different hall than where the princesses resided. He unrolled his shirt sleeves as he walked, pushing the cuffs back down and buttoning them.

He had another mission in mind today. And one didn't have an audience with the king in shirtsleeves. Inside the richly-appointed bedroom, he checked his black leather shoes for scuffs—none—and pulled the tie out of the top pocket of his suitcase, laid out on the foot of the bed.

Carrie had helped him pick it out. He'd confided in his sister before he and Alessandra had left the United States. She thought his plan to ask the king for Alessandra's hand before planning an extravagant proposal was romantic and perfect.

He wished he was as certain.

He stood before the bureau mirror, tucking the tie around his neck and knotting it.

In the past three months, he and Alessandra had been almost inseparable. He'd escorted her home a week after her near-fatal poisoning and met her older sister, Eloise. The king had been home, but the recent events had laid him up with an "episode," and Gideon hadn't had a chance to meet the man.

Gideon had stayed with Alessandra for nearly two months as the kingdom reeled from the attempts on their royal family. Had worked extensively with the security team, and although they hadn't discovered an inside man, their procedures had been sloppy, and the head of security had been happy to have Gideon as an advisor.

Then, they'd returned to the United States to the ranch. This time, with two of Alessandra's staff members as she worked on a proposal for a children's program that she'd been dreaming about for years. He'd had a few weeks to work with Nate and make some decisions about the ranch. Matt was back on active duty, and Gideon only had contact with him an occasional email and even rarer phone calls.

He and Alessandra had grown closer than ever. She'd been right that they could fit into each other's lives. He'd seen her nurturing spirit in the projects for which she chose to wield her influence. She made him laugh, made him notice the little things that he was often too busy to care about.

But there was still a part of him that worried things would fall apart. Something had happened between Carrie and Trey while he'd been in Glorvaird the first time, and although his sister had insisted that things were fine, he'd noticed the tension between them.

And while his feelings for Alessandra had deepened and grown...what if she wasn't ready for an engagement? What if she loved him, but she didn't want to marry him?

He knew there was protocol. That's why he was going to talk to her father first. But what if the man didn't approve? Gideon had no royal bloodlines. Although the ranch made a small profit most years, the real asset was their land. In no way was he considered rich.

Why in the world would the king agree?

But Gideon wasn't a coward, and he wasn't going to back down from this. He straightened the lapel of his suit jacket in the mirror and ran his comb through his hair once more—Alessandra had insisted he keep the beard—before gritting a frown and then turning for the door.

But before he left... He went to the suitcase once more and dug out the small, square jeweler's box he'd stowed beneath his drawers. For luck.

He'd had to work to convince the king's aide to give him the meeting, trusting the man with the real reason. Now he met the aide in the hall and followed the serious-faced fellow down another long hallway to a set of double-doors decorated with swirls of what might be real gold.

Gideon took one last deep breath as the doors swung open.

"You'll have a quarter hour," the assistant said in low tones as Gideon passed by him to enter the room.

The doors closed behind him.

The king sat behind a large cherry-wood desk ensconced in a fancy wheelchair. Alessandra had told Gideon what to expect when he eventually met her father—not knowing this was planned for today— but the man's wasted muscles and thinning white hair were still a shock. Gideon hid his reaction by bowing from the waist, the way he'd been instructed.

"Your Highness. Thank you for taking this meeting with me."

He straightened, meeting the King's stare. Though the man's body was failing him, there was no weakness in his shrewd gaze.

~ * ~

Alessandra sat across a small tea table from her older sister. Fine china and an elegant spread of pastries and fruit covered the white lacy tablecloth.

"So you're set on the American cowboy?"

Eloise wasn't one to mince words. Her sister's eyes met Alessandra's briefly and then skittered away. She didn't like to look at anyone in the face for very long. After years of being around her sister, Alessandra was used to it, though it still hurt.

Her sister's scars had never bothered Alessandra, not even when they'd been fresh and bright red, slashing across her cheek and neck, down into the shoulder of her blouses. But Eloise was incredibly sensitive about them.

She could also be incredibly rude.

"I love Gideon, yes," Alessandra answered.

Eloise picked apart the flaky pastry on her plate. "And I suppose you'll be spending a large amount of time in the States."

Alessandra frowned. She'd spoken to Eloise at-length after she'd arrived back in Glorvaird about her future plans. Eloise had agreed that she could cut back on some of her other events and take on some charity projects for children, ones that were close to her heart.

Was Eloise now thinking Alessandra would shirk her duties?

"We'll be spending some time at Gideon's home. His ranch has busy seasons where he's needed there."

Instead of acting upset, like Alessandra expected, Eloise nodded slowly. "Good. I have a project I need you to take on for me. It's very...sensitive."

Interest piqued, Alessandra leaned forward. "What kind of project?"

Eloise looked almost pained, if Alessandra had pegged her expression correctly. "This..." She shifted uncomfortably in her seat, and Alessandra had a moment of uncertainty. "Father recently confided in me that there was an infidelity when we were young."

Alessandra sat back in her seat, stunned. Of all the things she might've guessed, that wasn't one of them.

"There was a child. A daughter. Not legitimized, of course." Eloise looked down at the napkin in her lap. Alessandra still couldn't find words.

A sister. A half-sister.

"Her mother moved to America after the birth, and Father kept tabs on them for some time, but then the private investigator he'd hired lost them. Now, Father wants to find the girl. Before..."

Before he died. Alessandra's throat closed up. "I didn't think it was that close."

Eloise shrugged, her eyes on the window across. "The doctors say it might be as little as a year."

It wasn't nearly long enough. Being with Gideon had showed her that she could be brave enough to seek a deeper, reconciled relationship with her father, but... To only have such a limited time left brought a physical pain.

"Of course I'll help in whatever way I can," she said, a little hoarsely.

"I've two different investigators looking into finding her, but perhaps your man might have other contacts that would help."

Alessandra nodded. *Her man.* Yes, she'd enlist Gideon's help.

She wanted to get back to him now. To tell him of this new development. Talk through her muddled feelings about this revelation.

A sister.

~ * ~

When she found Gideon in the gardens, he seemed subdued. He glanced over his shoulder from where he stood near a stone bench in the rose arbor, and she saw his face was dark and brows were drawn. As she neared, she saw his suit jacket lying folded across one corner of the bench. And when he turned all the way around, she saw the tie he'd loosened around his neck.

She went to him and wrapped her arms around his waist. "What's the matter?"

She could feel the tension coiled in him, the tightness of his muscles.

"Nothing." His arms came around her upper back. He leaned back slightly, to better look into her face. "How was your sister?"

"Fine. I've got something to talk to you about." She squeezed his waist. "Later." And raised her face for his kiss.

He obliged her for a sweet kiss, but pulled away too soon.

"Something *is* the matter," she said with a slightly exaggerated moue. She reached up with one hand to touch his face, resting her palm against his cheek gently brushing with her thumb.

"No. I'm just...nervous."

"Nervous?" Her Gideon? Not likely. He broke their embrace and motioned for her to sit on the bench.

She humored him, perching on the edge of the cool stone. The scent of roses surrounded them and made the moment impossibly romantic. He stood tall, and she craned her neck to look up at him. One hand rested in his trouser pocket.

"I had everything planned perfectly for tonight, but...I don't think I can wait."

Then he dropped to one knee, and her stomach dipped. He reached for her with his empty hand, as his opposite hand brought a small black box out of his pocket. All her swirling thoughts stopped.

So did her breath.

"Alessandra, I love you. I can't imagine my life without you in it. Would you do me the honor of marrying me?"

She squeezed his hand tightly as tears blurred her vision. She blinked them back. "I love you, too. And...I'm so sorry to ruin your moment, but have you spoken to my father?"

One corner of his mouth tilted up. "Just this morning."

Her breathing eased. "And...? What did he say?"

"He gave his blessing."

She threw her arms around Gideon's neck, almost toppling them both. "Thank God."

She peppered his face with kisses until he took her

lips in a breath-stealing kiss. When they were both breathing hard, he pulled away and settled on the bench next to her.

"So that's a *yes*." It wasn't really a question, not the way he said it, slightly arrogant and more than a little relieved.

She leaned into his shoulder, watching as he pried open the black jeweler's box. "I would've married you anyway, without Father's blessing, but this makes it better..." Her thoughts, her words cut off as she caught sight of the ring. "Gideon..."

A large, sparkling diamond winked up at her, sunlight casting rainbows around it on Gideon's hands.

"It's too much." She didn't know the exact price tag, but a diamond like that must've cost his last two years' profits.

He cleared his throat. "I know we come from very different worlds, and I may never fit completely into yours, but I wanted to give you something fit for a princess."

He slipped it onto her finger, the metal cool against her skin. And because she was watching so closely, she noticed that his fingers were trembling.

She laced their fingers together, twisting the tangle of fingers to admire the darker tan of his skin against hers, and the sparkle of the ring.

"I love you," she said, looking into his dear face. "And *I'm* honored to be able to spend the rest of my life with you."

He steadied himself with a minute straightening of his shoulders, and she knew she'd said the right thing. Gideon might show the world a tough soldier, but she was the one who got to see the real man behind the facade.

That was the real treasure she valued. Gideon's heart.

ABOUT THE AUTHOR

USA Today bestselling author Lacy Williams works in a hostile environment (read: three-point-five kids age 6 and under). In spite of this, she has somehow managed to be a hybrid author since 2011, publishing 26 books & novellas. Lacy's books have finaled in the *RT Book Reviews* Reviewers' Choice Awards (2012, 2013, & 2014), the Golden Quill and the Booksellers Best Award. She is a member of American Christian Fiction Writers, Romance Writers of America and Novelists Inc.

F Williams Lacy
Williams, Lacy
Once upon a cowboy

43269895R00106

Made in the USA
San Bernardino, CA
17 December 2016